Evil Side of Money III: Redemption

By

Jeff Robertson

RJ Publications, LLC

Newark, New Jersey

The characters and events in this book are fictitious. Any resemblance to actual persons, living or dead is purely coincidental.

RJ Publications
mtymn19681@wowway.com
www.rjpublications.com
Copyright © 2009 by Jeff Robertson
All Rights Reserved
ISBN 0981777376
978-0981777375

Printed in the Canada

November 2009

1 2 3 4 5 6 7 8 9 10

Acknowledgements

First I would like to thank God to whom all praises are due forever…

I would like to thank my family for their support and sacrifice during this entire project; and for believing in it every step of the way.

Thank you to Richard Jeanty and the RJ Publications group for their faith and investment in this project also.

Thank you to all of my readers and fans for your support over the last 3 years. The encouragement you have given me has meant the world!!

Chapter 1

I remember waking up and vaguely hearing the news on the television about the Clinton and Lewinsky scandal. I remember having an excruciating headache, and being incredibly groggy. I also remember moving my legs and arms, making sure I wasn't paralyzed. I have always had a fear of that. I also remember moving them with the hope that they weren't cuffed or chained to the bed as a result of me being in "protective custody". I figured I was in a hospital, I knew that because of the smell. All hospitals have a distinctive smell. My next concern was Nate, I remember not buckling him in the back seat and I wondered whether or not he was injured. I turned my head gently not to aggravate my headache and I didn't see him in the room.

"Derrick, you're awake! Try not to move too much, you boys took a pretty bad spill out there," I remember a voice saying. It was Rev. Fisher; somehow he had gotten us into a hospital. He was there with his son and another lady.

"You're in a hospital Derrick, just relax and stay calm. You and your brother were involved in a bad accident," Fisher said.

"Rev. Fisher I am so glad you are here. Where's Nate?" I asked.

He looked at his son and the woman and motioned for them to leave the room, and they dutifully walked out. Rev Fisher pulled up a chair and sat next to the bed, folded his arms and crossed his legs.

"Derrick, are you feeling ok?" He asked.

"Yeah, my head hurts real bad, though," I whispered.

"The doctor said you suffered a concussion. Your head hit the steering wheel, son, you are blessed to be alive," Rev Fisher said in a fatherly tone.

Blessed was right, my head felt like someone had been hammering it all night! The nurse came in, introduced herself and gave me some pain medication. Rev. Fisher stood looking at me, seemingly studying me as I swallowed the medication. When the nurse left the room he took his seat back and assumed his previous posture.

"I have been praying for you boys since I found you on the highway. My son and I witnessed the entire accident; we had been in Chicago at a revival for the better part of the night and were on our way home when we saw you two. I called a few of my church members and we got you out of the car and into this hospital. We checked the two of you in under aliases, since we found no identification on you," he explained.

"Thank you Reverend, I really appreciate that, but you never answered my question. How is Nate?" I rebutted.

"Nathan suffered a concussion also, and he has a broken leg. He will be going to surgery when the doctors feel his concussion is under control. He is fine, he is in another room," Rev. Fisher explained. I was relieved; I was hoping that the police had not arrested him, or that Nate was not hurt in the accident.

"Derrick, I am going to ask you some questions, and I don't want you to lie to me you, understand? I stuck my neck out for you two and the least you can do is be honest with me," he said sternly. I nodded yes.

"What are you two involved in Derrick, what type of work do you do"? I turned my head to look out of the window.

"What do you mean, sir?" I asked.

"Don't be coy with me young man, you know exactly what I mean. You two crashed a two-hundred and fifty thousand dollar Bentley with a loaded gun in the car, I might add. The hospital drew you and your brother's blood and found large amounts of alcohol and marijuana in your systems to boot. What are you boys involved in?"

What was I gonna say? I had always respected Rev. Fisher and I didn't want to lie to him. At the same time, I couldn't tell him the truth either.

"I don't want to talk about it right now Reverend, I really cannot tell you," I said softly.

"Is that so? Well, maybe you might want to tell the police. They are right down the hall and they have been waiting to question you both. I, as well as the hospital staff, have kept them at bay, but since you don't want to talk to me, maybe you might want to talk to them instead".

"What do they want to talk to us about?" I asked nervously.

"I don't know, some explosion in New Lenox. A house exploded last night and they are questioning everyone," he said.

I knew what they wanted, I knew all about it. What was I going to do? Our backs were against the wall. I felt I could trust Rev. Fisher, but I felt ashamed to tell him the things we were into. And I didn't want to involve him, but we needed help. Everyone else was dead and I couldn't get to Nate to get his opinion. So I told him, not all of the details, but enough for him to give him an idea. As I told him, he just looked at me. I could see the disappointment on his face.

"What are you boys going to do now?" he asked.

"Honestly Reverend, I don't know," I lamented.

"Derrick, do you want to get out of this life?" he asked me.

"Yes, desperately, but I don't know what to do. I need help. Is it possible that you can help us?"

Evil Side of Money III: Redemption   *Jeff Robertson*

"Yes, we have a program for young men at our church ministry, but I will have to pray, meditate and ask God for direction on the issue. You and your brother's case pose challenges that I need help with," he said softly.

"All we need is another chance at life, I think my brother and I became victims of very severe circumstances and if we can get another shot at things I know we can turn our lives around," I said with confidence.

"Another chance at life is not my gift to give Derrick, it is God's. But if you pray sincerely, I am confident he will give you the direction and answers you search for."

My first obstacle would be Nate. The problem was Nate loved the life, and since all of our friends were killed as well as Gabby and the baby, I knew Nate would be out for revenge. I couldn't think of anything to say to him that would sway him from that. Things were different now, we had nothing to work with, and all of the Mafia guys were running for their lives from the police as well the Gangster Disciples. I'm sure all of our allies and resources were gone, what could he get revenge with? I let out a deep sigh and looked out of the window.

The pain medication they gave me was starting to wear off, so I paged for the nurse. After getting my meds, I reflected on our lives, we had spent just over ten years in the drug business and it had netted us nothing. All of the lives lost, money spent, and lives destroyed had come to me and Nate in a hospital room with all we had in the world in a suitcase. But at least we weren't dead or in jail......yet.

And that's where my hope came from. You see, as long as we were alive, I felt we could turn it around. We would have to make great sacrifices, but we could do it. Deep down I knew it would be an uphill battle, but very doable.

Later that evening after Rev. Fisher left, the nurse brought Nate into the room. "What's up, fool?" he said smiling.

"Nothing man, glad to see you are ok, though."

"Yeah, you can't drive for shit!" he said joking.

"How are you?"

"The doctor told me that I had a concussion, and my leg was fucked up pretty bad, but other than that I am ok."

After the nurse left the room, Nate looked at me and changed his tone.

"What the fuck is going on G, I heard the house blew up, what's up?" After I told Nate everything that happened during his two day high, he seemed despondent.

"Damn!" was all he replied.

After a few minutes of silence, he started lamenting over Gabby and baby Glo'. He began to sob and became very reflective, so I thought this might be a good time to give it to him, not all at once, but just a little.

"You know Nate, we are out of options, man, all of our people are gone, and we are on the run. I managed to grab us some money, but that's it. Now, I managed to get us some help to lay low for a while until we get our heads together. I don't know if you know it, but Rev. Fisher was the one who rescued us and got us in here under these aliases. He wants to help us, Nate, now he has this program at his church, and-"

I said before he cut me off.

"No.....fuck no! I don't like his ass, man. I ain't fucking with him, G! Plus, does it look like I am ready for prayer meeting? I just lost my wife and my baby girl, not to mention just about everything else I have in this world, now you got me going to the "Rev" so he can put me in heaven? That's your plan, G?" he asked me sarcastically.

"You got another one?" I asked slightly frustrated.

"Hell yeah, we can start by finding out who the fuck killed my family and the rest of our people and getting back on track! That's what we should be in here talking about, not no fucking church!" he said getting loud and agitated. I tried to compose myself through my slight headache. I really didn't want to meet his anger and intensity with some of my own, so I lowered my voice.

"Nate, number one, I don't know who killed Gabby, and the baby. I don't know who killed Dana, Mike, and Pete. Number two, we are in no position to try and find out, our best bet is to try to stay alive and out of jail ourselves right now. Number three there are no more resources, Nate, everything and everyone is gone; all we have in this world is in that suitcase and the clothes on our backs, that's it. Now, this preacher wants to give us a chance, Nate, a chance I think we should take. You fulfilled your dream, Nate, we were the gold standard when it came to selling drugs. The family was like the Roman Empire in Chicago and it was a good run, but it's over, Nate….it's over. Let it go, not many guys can go to the height that we did and live to tell about it. Let's take this chance, it might be our last," I said. He just looked at me long and hard before he responded.

"You know, that's easy for you to say, G, you ain't lost nothing…" he said before I cut him off.

"Fuck you man! Fuck you! I lost my life! I want a fucking life man! You had yours you did what you wanted to do! Now I want mine, I deserve that! I stuck by you, motherfucker, I did my part. Now I want my chance, I don't want this shit anymore!" I yelled.

I don't know what came over me, I guess the last ten years of emotion came out, the loss of family and loved ones. All of that penned up emotion just overflowed. After everything we had been through, all of our losses I could not believe Nate wanted to continue, I guess it was all too much for me to handle and I said things that I probably should have said seven to ten years earlier. Needless to say, with all of the yelling it wasn't long before the nursing staff came running in the room.

"What is going on in here? This is a hospital. You have to keep quiet or we will be forced to separate you two," the nurse said in a loud whisper.

I took a couple of deep breaths to cool down, and nodded to the nurse. Nate just sat there looking at me; I guess he couldn't believe I had talked to him that way. After the nurse left the room, I was ready for his rebuttal and his usual line of bullshit street logic and sarcasm. I was waiting for him to try and put a so-called logical street spin on the last ten years as he had done so often in the past. I was waiting and ready for anything he said or did, but he did nothing. He looked at me took in a deep breath, gently licked his lips cautiously turned over as not to hurt his bad leg, pulled the covers over his head and went to sleep. For the first time, I started to see my brother differently, I started to see him as an angry selfish man, who really only cared about himself. I started to see him as a spoiled ass Negro who felt the world owed him something because he grew up poor and had some bad breaks. For the first time, I started to see and believe that Nate was probably gonna end up where I had worked so hard to keep him from; in jail or dead. I started for the first time to entertain the thought that maybe my brother was not worth the risks that I had taken for him. I started to believe that for the last ten years my brother had duped me, and as much as it hurts to say.....he used me. I turned over through my exhaustion and growing headache and went to sleep.

The next day I was so tired, I woke up at twelve thirty in the afternoon. The nursing staff had already come in, prepped Nate for surgery on his leg and took him out. Rev. Fisher was standing by my bedside and asked me how I was doing.

"I guess I am ok Rev," I lumbered up from my bed and went in to use the bathroom. I remember being tired of dragging the IV pole every time I wanted to take a piss! I came out of the bathroom to find another nurse bringing me lunch. I had not recognized her from the previous two days and asked her what her name was, "Sandra," she replied.

"She is a member of my church Derrick, she had been on vacation and this is her first day back. Sandra this is Derrick, one of the young men I was telling you about," Fisher said, giving the informal intro.

"Nice to meet you," I said trying to close the back of my gown, as not to expose my ass.

"Here is your lunch, your brother is in surgery and will probably be there for another hour or so, and from there he will go to recovery. He will probably be back here by three-thirty or so," she said before leaving the room.

Sandra was a taller woman, about 5'8 or so, she had pretty long hair and a nice brown complexion with hazel eyes, a nice looking and mature woman I would say.

"How did everything go yesterday with Nathan?" Fisher asked.

"Not so good Reverend. I lost my temper with him, we argued," I said flatly.

"Well what was the conclusion; will he come to the church and start the program?" Fisher asked.

"There was no conclusion, we yelled, and went to sleep. I don't know what he's gonna do." Rev. Fisher pursed his lips and pulled up a chair and spoke to me in a fatherly tone.

"Derrick you have to let go, you have to stop carrying the burden of your brother's life, it's destroying your spirit. Your brother is a grown man, free to make his own decisions. God only holds us responsible for our lives and our decisions," he said.

"I thought you church folks taught that we are our brother's keeper," I said smiling.

"To an extent we do, but not necessarily in this case. If your brother is not ready for this, let him go and let him fulfill his own destiny. In time, maybe God will bring him around," he assured.

"I know Reverend, but I promised our mom that I would look after him, you know and-"

"And you have done a superior job, you have kept him alive and out of jail for the last ten years, now maybe it's your turn to start looking out for yourself Derrick."

He was right; I had been carrying the burden of Nate around like a bag of bricks for the past ten years or more. Maybe it's time now to set the bricks down. I made up my mind right there that if Nate didn't want to get into this program and turn his life around, I had to let him go and do it for myself. I loved my brother, but I had to start loving myself. After talking to Rev. Fisher for a while, he left and I fell asleep. I was awakened by the voices and movements of the nurse bringing Nate back into the room. I noticed he was still asleep as I peeked at him. I noticed they had his leg in traction, and heavily casted.

I was never one to be awakened and go immediately back to sleep, so I figured a little television would settle me back down. The local news was reporting that there was still an ongoing investigation into the explosion that leveled our compound. Detectives, firemen, and arson experts were saying that the occupants of the home had to be drug dealers because large amounts of burned money, and drug paraphernalia were found near and around the explosion. They went on to say that the bodies of many of the deceased were identified as known criminals with lengthy criminal records. I started to think it would only be a matter of time before the deaths of Mike, Dana, and Pete would be identified and the search for Nate and I would begin.

Nate woke me up at about 1 p.m. asking the same stupid question we all ask people who are obviously asleep.

"Hey G, you sleep?"

"I was. What's up?" I replied.

"I been thinking man, and I wanted to talk to you about some things."

"What is it, Nate?" I asked slightly agitated.

"Well, first I want to say I'm sorry for snapping at you. I am still fucked up by the loss of my baby girl and Gabby. We lost a lot in the last few days and I am just not dealing with it well. And even though I don't really like this dude, I am willing to try your plan for going over there and hiding out for a while. Maybe some religion might do me some good. You were right man, you did stick by me and protected my ass, you're my brother for life and I owe you, I realize that. The shit just aint gonna be easy for me," he confided.

"Nate, it's cool, man, don't worry about it. Let's just go with Rev. Fisher and get our heads together."

"Yeah, maybe after a while things can get back to the way they were before all of this shit happened," Nate said.

Nate just didn't understand; I didn't want to go over to Rev. Fisher's church to hide out for a while; I wanted to make a complete change. And things were never going to be like they were. We were on the run now. We were running from the police and our past, a sprint many people never win. But I didn't care, as long as he consented to go, time will take care of all of his misconceptions. Nate deciding to go was a huge load off my mind, and I couldn't wait to tell Rev. Fisher.

Rev. Fisher was elated that God had changed Nate's heart about going into the program at his church, so was I. I had almost recovered from my concussion, and we were probably gonna be released soon. Nate's leg was healing fine and he seemed to be really relaxed about our decision, but he was still angry and defiant. He was angry about giving up the life, angry about Gabby and baby Glo's death, angry about Dana and the crew, angry about everything and at everybody. After our discussion he would never vent his anger toward me, so he took it all out on the nursing staff and Rev. Fisher. Not long after I told Rev. Fisher about Nate's decision that he decided to come up to the hospital to see if Nate had warmed up to him. It was a disaster!

"Nathan, I am glad you will be joining us at the church, all of the members look forward to meeting you and Derrick," Fisher said.

"How many members you got, Rev, about eight or nine?" Nate asked sarcastically.

"No, we have about one hundred and fifty on register, but our faithful make up about sixty or seventy."

"I don't know why they are so interested in meeting me, I ain't no church man or nothing," Nate said shifting his injured leg.

"I told them about you and Derrick, and everyone is excited about you two joining our men's group," Fisher said smiling.

"Yeah, out here in the sticks, they probably ain't had too much to get excited about lately! Look, I aint going out there to be no guinea pig or nothing! I don't want no church folks looking at me and laughing, I ain't no damn clown!" Nate said agitated.

"Don't talk to my pastor that way!" Nurse Sandra said walking into the room. Nate sunk back down into the bed and shifted his leg once again and looked away in disgust.

"You haven't touched any of your breakfast, Nathan, when do you plan on eating?" she asked with concern.

"I'll eat it when I get hungry," Nate said angrily.

"Fine then, don't eat it! You're an arrogant angry person, all of us are just trying to help you and-" Sandra said before the Reverend cut her off.

"Sandra, it's ok. Leave his food. We'll take care of it," Sandra slammed the plate down and stormed out of the room. I just shook my head in disgust, I was completely embarrassed.

"Nathan, may I talk to you for a moment, alone?" Fisher asked.

"Whatever Rev," Nate said sarcastically. I picked up my robe, slippers and IV pole and went into my pocket to get some change. I figured this would be a good time to sneak down to the vending machine and get some candy.

"Nathan, I understand your fear and anger. I want you to grow and someday give your life to Christ and fulfill God's will for you, and I am willing to suffer that it may be so. But I am very protective of the people God has trusted me with, and however rude you are to me, I will not allow you to mistreat God's children. Do you understand?" he said sternly.

"Now that we have that understanding, I want to tell you something. I know what you boys were involved in, Nathan, and you are perfectly free to return to that life. I am in no way pressuring you to come to the church, but if you do, you will be respectful. You two have been involved in ugly and heinous crimes and there may still be time to redeem yourselves, but you have to want it, Nathan, and you're gonna have to work for it. Now Christ offers you a free love gift of salvation, but your redemption to mankind is going to take some work. You have two days to think about the rest of your life, Nathan, two days to look at the crossroad and make a decision. You have already been down one path; you know what it holds for you. Make your mother proud, Nathan, and choose the right path," Rev. Fisher said.

"Just what are you saying, man?" Nate said confused and irritated.

"I am saying this day God has presented you with two choices, death and life. I strongly urge you to choose life," Rev. Fisher said.

For the next few days, Nate really didn't say much. He was still rude to the nursing staff, but he was pretty quiet.

Once in a while I would catch him staring off looking out the window. In the past, Nate often told me that the two things he feared the most was jail and a job. Now I found out something else Nate was terrified of... the future. You see, looking back, I understand it all. Nate was an animal and the street was his jungle where he ruled, but now he was about to be taken out of his element and placed into one he didn't understand, much less rule. He understood the street rules and creed, the hustler and gangster life, but life as a squared guy was foreign to him. As Nate looked on to our exodus from the street life with fear, I looked at it with cautious optimism.

CHAPTER 2

January 23rd, 1998 was the date of our discharge from the hospital. Nate's leg had healed, and he was now able to get around on crutches. That day began our new life, a life without drugs, and murder. But that day started for me with a grim reminder of what had been. The local news reported that police had apprehended Jonathan W. Mullenrand, of the powerful Mullenrand banking family. Local, state, and federal officials had charged Jon with being the head of the most powerful drug distribution families in the state, and possibly the region. They had Jon on conspiracy, drug distribution, extortion, murder, racketeering, and a whole lot more. They slammed him with somewhere in the neighborhood of forty or fifty felony counts. Authorities had claimed he was the mastermind of the whole outfit, and had tied him to most of the gangland killings in the area.

Mike and Dana were also mentioned and were accused of being his lieutenants, and enforcers. The local news had shown a hierarchy chart like the ones they used to use to show mafia chain of command, and had placed Jon at the top as the leader. They showed Jon getting out of an unmarked police car with his hands cuffed, wearing a bullet proof vest and surrounded by police officials. I remember looking at him and barely being able to recognize him.

Jon looked as if he had lost about twenty pounds! He looked battered, unkempt and extremely tired. At that moment, I felt an enormous amount of sorrow for him. Jon was unable to commit most of the crimes they had slammed on him, but somehow he was taking the fall. I wasn't really sure whether or not he had ratted us out, and at this point it didn't matter. He was about to spend the rest of his life in prison while Nate and I walked free. The guilt I felt was tremendous. I pulled Nate into the bathroom at the hospital and told him what I had seen.

"Damn, they got Jon. You think he will rat us out?" Nate asked me.

"I don't know, Nate, Jon probably doesn't even know we are alive," I lamented.

"Well that's great. That's cool, G. Shit, maybe we will get away with this after all. Wow that's ironic man, Jon didn't even know about half the shit we did in the family. Oh well, that's life," Nate said casually.

"That's life, is that all you have to say? This guy is going to die in jail for crimes he didn't even commit! He's taking the fall for us and you say that's life?" I exclaimed.

"G, you're right, Jon didn't commit those crimes, but he wasn't innocent either. If they only charged Jon with the crimes he did commit he would still probably do life in a federal pen, so what's the difference? Mail fraud, bank fraud, money laundering, and conspiracy are all felonies, G, don't get this shit twisted. Jon bankrolled the whole operation with stolen money, and helped us launder about forty million dollars around the area, so don't feel too sorry for him," Nate said.

Nate was right, life in prison was life in prison, and the charges are pretty much interchangeable. Still, I felt sorry for him and I missed him. I had always wondered what had happened to Jon during those fateful two days. I guess the authorities had picked him up somewhere and hauled him in for questioning. Jon probably did rat us out and told them where we lived, but I forgave him. God only knows what he had gone through in those following weeks. My mind began to wander and I started to reflect on the crew, and all of the things we had done, I couldn't believe Nate and I had been allowed to escape relatively unscathed. Which begs the question, why? Why had we been allowed to escape? Obviously the powers that destroyed us knew about us, and then there was the strange talk of Detective Trent on his death bed. His strange talk that "they" were coming to get us, who were "they?" I felt it was time to confront Nate about all of my lingering questions.

"Nate, let me ask you a question. Was there ever anyone else involved in our operation?" I asked casually.

"What do you mean?"

"You know, like a go-between. You see earlier that night that all of the shit went down at the house, I went to the hospital and talked to Trent and-"

"You did what? I told you, G, not to talk to that motherfucker about anything! What did he tell you?" Nate said agitated.

"Nothing really, just a lot of off the wall talk people coming to the house to get us, and that these people knew where we were and stuff. You know anything about that?"

"Who knows what that motherfucker was talking about, he had cancer, G, and he was probably on medication and out of his head. Anyway, I don't want to talk about it. I got enough shit on my mind than to talk about his ass!" Nate said angrily.

I knew he was lying. He simply dismissed the conversation to keep from having to tell the truth. There was something he was not telling me. Since it was supposed to be a day of new beginnings I tabled the situation, but I would ask him again....soon.

Rev. Fisher arrived and helped us get all of our things together and signed us out under the church's care. My biggest worry was Nate, and how he would take to the whole situation. He was still bitter and very angry about baby Glo and Gabby.

"You boys will be staying at the church the time being, we have the upstairs all ready for you and some of the congregation is waiting to welcome you," Fisher said gleefully.

"Whatever man, look we aint gonna have to sing no hymns and shit today, are we? Cause I aint up for it," Nate said sarcastically.

"Hey Nate, why don't you relax, man?" I said

I could tell that Rev. Fisher was offended; if he was going to help Nate it was going to take all of his patience and some divine help to boot. Soon, Rev. Fisher's son Jeremiah and some of the other members came in to put our stuff in the car. Nurse Sandra came in also to tell us goodbye and give us our discharge papers.

"I will be seeing you two soon at church, I hope. And you make sure you keep eating, Nathan," she said with a sly smile. I think she kind of liked Nate. They went back and forth constantly about his eating and meds. Some of the other nurse staff would get together and talk about how protective she was of him and how she took a "special" interest in him. I shrugged the whole notion off; Nate had way too many issues for a woman like her. I remember walking out of the hospital and looking around for the cops. I was always nervous about that. That's one of the problems of being a former criminal, you spend your life looking for the time when all you have done comes to a head. Deep inside, every criminal knows what goes around comes around, and eventually he will have to pay the piper, but he never knows when or how.

During the drive, Nate didn't say a word; he just stared out of the window. From time to time he would adjust his injured leg and grimace from discomfort, but that was it. We drove through some of the rough areas of Joliet, past the prison and around Jefferson Street until we got to an area near Bicentennial park not too far from Evergreen apartments. That area was rough, but it wasn't anything that Nate and I weren't used to.

As we pulled in front of the church, my first impression wasn't great. There was a small lot in front of the church with a couple of wrecked cars and a beat up old school bus they were using for church transportation. I could tell someone had been trying to do some gardening around the church but it wasn't working out too well. The church itself was huge and pretty shabby. The building looked old and hollow. Nate looked at me and whispered "Is this it?"

"Yeah I think so," I whispered back.

"Fuck this, take me back to Chicago," Nate said in disgust.

"You know we can't go back there, Nate, just make the best of it," I said.

Rev. Fisher got out and opened Nate's side of the car door and extended a hand to help him out. "Well boys, this is it, it isn't much but it's still God's house. We're making repairs as we go along."   I didn't know what to say. Looking at Rev. Fisher's face, I could see that he was quite proud of the building. He gave us a tour of the church; the kitchen, the sanctuary, the side rooms they used for meetings and classes, and finally upstairs where Nate and I would be staying. When we got to the door, he flung it open and there were four older women inside that had hung some decorations and made a cake to welcome us to the church. Everyone yelled "surprise" and they all hugged us and gave us kisses to welcome us to the church family.

We ate cake and drank coffee and tea for about an hour. We got acquainted with some of the church mothers without giving any details; they didn't mind, I don't think they cared to know too much anyway. Rev. Fisher just beamed with pride, I could tell he wanted to just jump for joy that Nate and I had come there. I must say I enjoyed everything too, the people were very nice, It was evident they really cared about us. There was only one problem though; I didn't see any of the other guys that were supposed to be in the ministry with us.

"Uh, excuse me, ma'am, where are the other guys?" I asked.

"What other guys?"

"You know, the other guys that will be in the ministry with us."

"Sweetie, you two are it, I know of no other guys," she said humbly.

That was my first lesson about some people in the church; they have the tendency to make things seem more than what they really are. Rev. Fisher and his people gave me the impression that it was an existing ministry, that there were guys already involved. I had no idea Nate and I were the "guinea pigs." It really didn't matter to me though; I just wanted a new start in life. If it had to be this way, it was okay with me. Nate on the other hand was a different situation all together.

"This is some bullshit G, he lied to us! I told you he aint shit," Nate said angrily.

"Hey, watch your mouth man we are in a church!" I said

"I don't give a shit, this place gives me the creeps anyway! And these people, man, what is this some kind of cult or some shit?"

"Nate, chill man, these people are trying to help us, man. Don't forget what we are in this for," I cautioned.

"Help my ass! They got us up in this drafty ass attic like we some slaves or something! I don't like it."

"Would you prefer jail? Look Nate, it aint the best, I agree, but it's all we got right now. If we go back to Chicago, we'll end up in jail or dead. Like it or not, this is it for us right now, we are out of options." Nate looked at me for a second and slumped down into the chair. He knew I was right, he knew whatever he felt about the situation was irrelevant. He had to make the best of it. Then Rev. Fisher knocked at the door.

"Boys, after you get cleaned up I would like to see you in my office, okay?" he asked.

"Sure, we'll be down as soon as we finish, sir," I said. Nate rolled his eyes in disgust.

I stood in the middle of the room with my hands on my hips and took a survey of our room. Two beds, a couple of dressers for our clothes, two nightstands, a black and white television, and a bathroom for Nate and I to share. That was it. We also noticed a small leak in the ceiling dripping into a pot on the floor.

"Look at this shit. A couple of months ago I was sleeping in a king sized bed, satin sheets with an ounce of weed and a bottle of V.S.O.P on the nightstand. Now I'm in this rat hole living like a fucking indentured servant!" Nate said in disgust.

I shook my head, he just didn't get it. However, this time I did agree with him. A glass of Cognac would have been good right about now.

Later that night after a hearty meal cooked by one of the church mothers, Rev. Fisher, Nate and I assembled in his office to talk. "Well boys, what do you think?" he asked.

"You don't want to know what I think," Nate said rolling his eyes. Rev. Fisher looked at him and forced a smile.

"What about you, Derrick?"

"Uh, it's okay, sir. I like it okay," I said mildly. Rev Fisher gave me an approving smile.

"Good, because this is your home. This is where you will be living until the end of the program, which is what I asked you two up here to discuss. On the streets there are laws, street laws and codes that you have to follow to survive, am I right?" he asked.

"Yeah, sure," I answered.

"No different here. There will be no profane language, no drinking or drug use, and no female visitations. You are not to leave unless you are accompanied by a member of our staff. The phone in your room has been fixed so that you cannot receive any calls, however you may make calls out, and those will be monitored. I have prepared a work schedule for you two to do various duties around the church. You will be paid a respectable wage, and it will be deposited into an account for you both. I will give you two bible classes three times a week and Sunday services are mandatory for you both. Are we clear?" he said firmly.

"Hey man, what is this all about?" Nate asked

"It's about something you have never had in your life, boy, structure, discipline, boundaries, responsibility, and accountability. Now you don't have to abide by these rules, you can walk out of that door and never look back. I won't try to stop you, but I guarantee you, in six months you both will be dead or in police custody. Today I present to you both, life or death, the choice is yours, but I suggest you choose life," he said plainly.

"What if it doesn't work out Rev. Fisher, what if we are beyond help?" I asked.

"Son, no one is beyond the help of God if they want it. God has given you two a second chance, a chance at redemption, and he has a plan for your lives."

"How do you know all of that?" Nate asked sarcastically.

"You two have committed unspeakable crimes, and have been allowed to walk away from it all relatively unscathed, how do you account for that? How do you account for not being killed in that accident? How do you account for the police believing you to be dead and really not looking for you? How do you account for the help of me and this congregation, maybe just coincidence, huh? Get up both of you and walk over to the window and look out. What do you see? Drunks, prostitutes, gang bangers, and all types of indigents, right? The only difference between them and you is that you want God's help and they don't. Jesus once said whosoever hungers and thirsts after righteousness shall be filled. You know what the most powerful word in that statement is-whosoever. Some people don't want God's help; they would rather try and do it on their own. Boys, you will find that all along life's journey there are choices, some choices are more important than others, some have longer lasting consequences than others."

"Yeah, but why we gotta go through all of this shi-, I mean stuff?" Nate asked.

"Of course, you know some people want the whole world but they don't want to go through anything to get it. Some people want education, but they don't want to go to class. Some want fine homes and fancy cars, but don't want to pay for them. Some want children, but don't want to provide for them. It seems nowadays everyone wants a free ride. Well boys, nothing is free, anything worth having carries a cost."

"But you said last week at the hospital that salvation was a free gift," I interjected.

"It is free for you; Jesus paid the price for your sins and salvation. It's a free gift for you, but believe me there was a heavy burden carried for you to have such a precious choice."

"I'm not sure I understand, sir," I said.

"Don't worry; you'll understand it all in due time. Well boys it's getting late what will it be, death or life?" he asked.

"I'll stay, sir," I said. He looked at Nate for his response.

"I'll stay man," Nate said begrudgingly.

"Good, then I'll see you at eight in the morning, bright and early."

"Hey, why so early?" Nate asked.

"Oh, I'm sorry. That's another law around here; no one sleeps past eight o'clock."

That night, lying in bed, I thought long and hard about some of the things Rev. Fisher said to us. I hadn't heard such things since mamma Williams died, I knew Nate hadn't either. Nate used to talk about surviving in the streets, but Rev. Fisher talked about surviving in life. Nate didn't say much after our talk; he and I cleaned up and drifted off to sleep. In the middle of the night I was awakened by mumbling and loud talk and noises. Nate was having a nightmare apparently, so I woke him up.

"Man, you okay?" I asked.

"Uh, yeah. Just another nightmare," he said still groggy.

"What about?"

"About Gabby and the baby, I dreamed they were drowning and I couldn't save them. No matter how hard I tried I just couldn't save them. Man G, I miss them so much. There's so much I want to say to them, so much I want to do. I should be out there trying to find out who killed them, instead I'm up in here doing this church shit," he said getting angry.

"Nate, relax it's going to be okay, man, we're gonna find out who did it, don't worry."

"How, G, laying up in here? I hate this fucking place. I don't think I want to do this shit G. Let's just go man, he said he wasn't gonna stop us!"

I looked long and hard at Nate and something in me knew it was time. It was time to stand up and draw a line with my brother.

"You want to go?" I asked.

"Hell yeah."

"Then go, I'm staying. You talk about going, but you never can tell me where. You know why? Cause there ain't nowhere to go, Nate. We got criminals and police looking for us. The last place they would think to find us is here, the way I see it, I ain't been safer since I was in the womb!" I said convincingly. Nate picked up the lamp and threw it against the wall in a fit of rage.

"Great Nate, now what are we gonna do for light?" I asked.

"I don't give a fuck! I feel trapped in this motherfucker!"

It was good that it was dark, so he couldn't see my smile. Now he knew how I felt for over ten years in the drug game...trapped! I turned over and went to sleep. The next morning I was awakened by the smell of good breakfast food. I glanced at the clock through tired eyes and noticed it was shortly after seven in the morning. My back was to Nate's side of the room and I was afraid to look over to see if he had left in the night. Wow, I thought he made it through the first night. He was lying in the bed with the covers all over the floor and his head back with his mouth open. I smiled at him and took advantage of his sleep and got in the shower first. When I got out, he was up and making up his bed still with a scowl on his face.

"You up, huh?" I asked.

"Yeah, that fat broad came up here talking about the food was ready."

"Smells good, huh?"

"Yeah, but how is it gonna taste?"

We were both startled by a knock at the door. It was Rev Fisher letting us know breakfast would be served in about ten minutes. When we arrived downstairs, I noticed there were a lot more people there than I expected. Later, I found out that once a month Rev. Fisher meets with the leadership of the church and has breakfast to discuss things. This particular morning the topic of conversation was Nate and I. As it turned out Rev. Fisher's idea of a men's ministry was met with a little opposition, namely from the Deacon Board. Having known our past, the leadership felt apprehensive about committing to something that would require so much of the church's time or resources. Also, the chairman of the Deacon board felt it should be up to the church to decide or vote on the ministry, not solely Rev. Fisher.

At this discussion was the Chairman of the Deacon Board Otis Jackson. Jackson had been with Rev. Fisher since he started the church. Jackson was a hard liner who felt that the church should be run the way it was in the old days. He also felt that the Pastor of any church was simply a hired servant, and it was the job of the Deacon board to act as a spokesman of the congregation. Jackson was a dark skinned hard looking little man from Mississippi. He looked to me to be in his sixties with mingled grey hair and a deep voice. He spoke very slowly and with stern conviction. He and his wife wielded a lot of power in the small congregation, and their opinions were highly regarded.

Sitting directly across from Jackson was Mother Vincent. Mother Vincent was a jolly happy-go-lucky woman also from Mississippi. She looked to be also in her sixties with a wonderful personality. She was the church's head mother and did most of the cooking as she did this particular morning. She was a woman whose loyalty was with whatever was good for the entire church. She seemed to be in favor of the ministry, but felt Rev. Fisher should have given the church more time to consider all that would be involved and required.

Then there was Sandra Jackson, the nurse from the hospital; she was the church's chief trustee. She loved Rev. Fisher and went along with whatever he felt was good for the church. She completely trusted his judgment and loved him like a father, so needless to say he had her vote. Rev. Fisher's son rounded out the group. Jeremiah was a heady young guy a little younger than Nate and I. He was the only other minister in the church, and was about to be sent to the seminary to study. Rev. Fisher knew he was getting older and wanted to prepare his son to take over the ministry after he was gone. I guess with Rev. Fisher's cancer scare he decided to speed things up a little with his son's progress.

"Reverend, I just believe that this is not the right time for a ministry of this magnitude. We are stretched way too thin as it is," Jackson said.

"Brother Jackson, I understand your concern, but God has spoken to me about these two young men and I think it would be the right time. I believe God will supply any needs we have. We are in the business of soul saving brother deacon, and that is what this is all about," Fisher said.

"I'm all for soul winning, I just think this is ill timed, that's all."

"How much do we have allotted for this ministry, Reverend?" Vincent asked.

"I don't operate that way Sister Vincent. I move on God's command. God told me to start this ministry with these two boys, and to operate in a spirit of faith. How can I do that if I start counting money?"

"Well, let's just pray that God will bless us with all that we need and go with it. We all know Reverend is a man of God, let's just trust and support him," Sandra said.

I couldn't believe they were discussing us while we were sitting right there, but that was also part of Rev. Fisher's policy. He believed in everything being done on the table and up front. He never liked closed door meetings, he always said it threatened the spirit of transparency he wanted for the church. Also, he believed closed door meetings gave way to gossip. He wanted everyone to know what was being said and by whom. The only times I ever remember Rev. Fisher having closed door meetings were if he was counseling, everything else was wide open.

"Well, we have to agree people if we are going to take this to the congregation. So, let's make our decision now by vote of majority. If we vote no, the boys must leave, if yes we will go on as planned. But remember, you are voting on these boys' future, so vote your conscience and let God's love lead you," Fisher warned. By a show of hands the majority voted for us to stay. Fisher, Sandra, Vincent, and Jeremiah all voted yes. Deacon Jackson voted no. I couldn't understand why Jackson was so adamant about us leaving, I must admit from that point on, I started to dislike him. How could anyone vote to throw two young men out on the street and claim to be a Christian, I thought?

"It's settled, the boys will stay. And to show just how certain I am that this is the move of God, I am going to pay for this ministry with my own money," Fisher announced.

"You don't have to do that Reverend, we have voted. The church will support the ministry," Sandra said.

Everyone agreed, but I understood why he was doing it. First, he didn't want to stretch the church's finances too thin, and he really believed in what he was doing and wanted to show Nate and me he did too. I didn't know about Nate but I didn't intend on letting the Rev. Fisher down.

Our typical day consisted of a hearty breakfast, a work detail (usually something around the church) and a class. That usually rounded out the morning into the early afternoon. After lunch, we would start the process over, but backward; A class, a work detail, and dinner. Lights out was usually about nine o'clock. The first couple of weeks were rough, especially for Nate who wasn't used to doing much of anything. It wasn't long before he started to nag me like he did when we worked at McDonalds. He was constantly pissed off. He would complain about the work details, the food, the classes, and the people. My only problem was that I was always tired. Between Nate's poison nightmares and his constant complaining during the day, I never got any rest.

One day Rev. Fisher decided to separate us. Nate was given a detail that required him to go to a local hardware store with Deacon Jackson, and I was given the job of painting the men's and women's bathrooms. I knew no one would be back for at least an hour, so I decided to sneak a snooze. Walking upstairs to the bedroom I glanced out of one of the windows and was startled to see an unmarked car sitting downstairs while a man on the inside snapped pictures from the drivers' side. He didn't notice me, so I went downstairs to take a closer look.

The man looked to be in his early thirties, blonde, wearing dark sunglasses. He seemed to be oblivious to the passersby as he snapped away furiously with his small camera. The car he drove was a late model Ford or Lincoln with no license plates on the front and the ones on the back were slightly obscured. As he snapped his last picture he stopped one of the pedestrians on the street, an older woman and began talking to her.

I was gesturing toward the church. Clearly, he was asking about it. The woman shook her head no a couple of times and yes once or twice more, and walked away. Afterward, the man rolled up his window and sped off. I darted out of the church when he was out of sight and looked for the woman. Being older she hadn't gotten too far up the street.

"Hello ma'am my name is Donald and I am a member of that church across the street may I ask you what that guy was saying to you?" I asked.

"Nothin' really, he wanted to know if I attended the church, and if I knew the pastor that's all," she said nervously.

"Well, what did you tell him?"

"I told him I didn't, and I don't know the pastor. What is all of this about young man?" The woman asked curiously.

"Nothing, he was probably a bill collector or something, you know how it is," I said leisurely.

Now I was really concerned. Who the hell was this guy? Could he have been looking for Nate and me? Could he have been that third party that Detective Trent spoke of on his deathbed? Maybe I was overreacting, maybe he knew Reverend Fisher or something, but if he did, why didn't he just come into the church and ask for him, and what the hell was he taking pictures for? Later that night, I talked it over with Nate.

"What did he look like, G?" Nate asked slightly worried.

"I don't know, white boy, early to mid thirties, blonde hair. Why? You know him?" I asked.

"Nah, maybe he knows Fisher or somebody in the church."

"That's what I thought at first, but if so, why didn't he just come in and ask for whomever he was looking for?"

"You think he was the police?"

"Shit who knows man, right now all of the wrong people are looking for us, who can tell." I said.

"And he was taking pictures huh?" Nate said reflectively.

"Yeah....is there something you want to tell me Nate, something maybe you forgot to mention?"

"No, why?"

"It's just that there's been a lot of strange shit going on ever since I talked to Trent in the hospital, and-

"I don't want to talk about that shit tonight G, let it go!"

"That's exactly what I mean, every time I try to talk to you about what went down you always hush me up. You hiding something?"

"No man, now let it go!" he said agitated.

"Fuck you Nate, don't be hiding nothing from me man, whatever you into I want to know cause my ass is on the block right with yours! I don't like that shit man let me know what is going on!" I shouted.

Once he saw that he wasn't going to be able to brush me off as easily as in the past, he calmed down and came over and sat next to me on the couch. He took a deep breath and spoke softly and quietly.

"G, there's a lot I can't tell you, at least not right now. I'm gonna hip you up, just give me some time to get shit straight in my head and about who killed my family ok? I promise I will tell you everything." he said trying to reassure me.

"Ok, man but just don't forget-

"I won't. I promise."

Chapter 3

Reverend Fisher spent a lot of time with us teaching us about Jesus and the scriptures, and how we should live our lives. I must say, even Nate was interested; I noticed he asked questions often and sometimes would even give input. He still wasn't buying into the whole church thing, though. Nate felt all religion was a scam, man's way of controlling people. When Nate voiced this opinion, Reverend Fisher blew us away with his response.

"Nate, you are absolutely right, and I agree with you," he said casually.

"You do?" Nate asked shocked.

"Absolutely, Religion is man's way of controlling each other. But what I am teaching you boys about is not religion, it is about relationship. A relationship with your creator; let me give you an example. Nathan, is it possible for you to know a person without being close to them?"

"Yeah, I remember when I had the family I used to tell them not to let anybody in and don't get close to nobody," Nate explained.

"That's right, you can talk to people, hang out with them even, and never allow them to get close, never really get to know them. Never establish a relationship with them, right?"

"Yeah, but what you driving at Rev?" Nate asked.

"That's the way it is with many people and God. They spend time at his house, which is the church. They talk to him, which is called prayer, they even socialize with him and his family, which is called fellowship, and never really know him," Fisher explained.

"That's deep," I said.

"It's not deep, it's called religion," Fisher said.

"Well how do you get to really know him then?" Nate asked

"The same way you get close to anyone else, Nathan, you let them in. You let them into your heart. You share your inner most thoughts and fears with him. You spend intimate quiet time with him; you learn of his ways, you live to please him. In short, you let him into your life."

Nate looked around trying to let it all soak in. He looked up at the cracked ceiling, scratched his head and spoke.

"How can you do all of that with something that you can't see, I would feel stupid," Nate said.

"Just because you can't see God with your eyes doesn't mean he is not there, Nathan," Fisher reasoned.

"What? Nah man, if I can't see it, it aint there," Nate said confidently.

"Are you sure?" Fisher asked with a slight grin.

"Yeah man, of course."

"I'll make a wager with you, Nathan, if I prove you wrong, you have to wash the church bus tomorrow morning, without Derrick's help, but if I can't, you get a week off from chores. Is it a deal?"

"Humph, yeah man."

"Good. Tell me, Nathan, when is the last time you've seen the wind?"

"All the time man, when the trees are bent over and paper flying all around-

"No, that is the effects of the wind, but you have never seen the wind itself. No one has. The trees bending, paper flying, the feeling of it blowing onto your skin is evidence that it is there but you have never seen it. When you go to the hospital and they give you an X-ray do you feel anything, do you see anything, do you smell anything?"

"Well, no."

"But when the radiologist brings out the picture you see the bones in your hand, right? How do you account for that Nathan?"

"I....don't know."

"There are forces, very strong forces in the universe that are invisible, but make themselves known through the visible. Gravity, have you seen it, can you touch it, can you smell or taste it? Yet when you throw something in the air it comes right back down. That's the force that makes it happen, yet if you go so many miles outside of the earth's atmosphere the force of gravity no longer exists. God is real Nathan; he is only waiting for you to make him real in your heart."

Nate and I both sat there in amazement. We had heard preaching before, and we had heard about people getting the "Holy Ghost" and running around and foaming at the mouth, but no one had ever talked to us about making God real in our hearts and how we should live for him.

"End of the lesson for tonight boys, it's late. Nate, Mother Vincent will let you know where the bucket and soap is for the church bus in the morning," Fisher said smiling.

The next morning, Nate and I really didn't say much to each other about our talk the previous night; I guess enough had already been said. Rev. Fisher decided to split Nate and me that morning. Rev. Fisher and Deacon Jackson took Nate to the hardware store to pick up a few things. I stayed behind to start painting. I remember being sort of happy Nate went along with them, I really wasn't up for Nate's complaining and belly-aching.

Walking past the huge window of the church facing the street, I noticed a man once again sitting in a late model Ford snapping pictures of the front of the church. He looked to be in his mid thirties also, with blonde hair and dark glasses. He snapped away furiously and spoke into a hand-held recording device. Once again I began to worry, who the hell were these guys and why were they staking out the church?

Something was definitely wrong, but I wanted to do my own investigating before talking to Nate.

We began our day of painting and cleaning, I really didn't mind it at all. It gave me a chance to reflect on things and think about how lucky we were not to have been caught by the police. We had our classes around mid day, worked a little more, and ended the day with another class. I must say the teaching that Rev. Fisher gave us was interesting, but I wasn't buying much of it, it was just something different. As the weeks went by, Nate began to get more interested in the teachings; I must admit it was surprising. He asked more and more questions, and read more and more of the bible. I remember one night he was reading from the book of Proverbs, and he actually started to get excited.

"You know, G, this stuff is cool, you know it aint bad."

"Oh yeah, how so?"

"Well, this guy Solomon was a king and all, and he got some teachings in here that are true you know. Some of the stuff I used to say when we had the family, but you know differently."

I enjoyed watching him talk about what he had read, as he went on and on, my mind went back to a certain situation we went through when we had the family. Remembering the situation and how Nate handled it amazed me at how this is the same man sitting in front of me now talking about King Solomon.

April 1990

"Well, I'll tell you what the motherfucker is gonna have to go about the shit the way we do things, G, you know the family way."

"I know Nate but he ain't that kind of guy you know, he wants to get in the game but he's doing it out of necessity."

"I could give a damn, we still got a way to do things around here, you know."

"Ok, whatever. Tell me what it is you want me to tell him."

"Tell him we will give him a strip to sell on Cottage Grove, if he does well then we will promote his ass."

"How much you gonna trust him with?"

Nate sat twirling his cigar in his mouth thinking. "Give him a kilo, see how he handles that."

"Nate you are talking about a man that has no experience in the drug game, he's trying to make ends meet. For all intense and purposes he's a squared guy just trying to put food on the table and you're gonna trust him with a kilo of coke?"

"How much experience did we have? And besides, a kilo ain't that much. Give it to him but let him know that if he fucks up, I'll kill him, family or no family."

"Nate, I think that's a mistake. Maybe we should let him work with one of the regimes, get to know the game a little giving him that much this soon-"

"G, are you running this shit or am I? Give him the kilo and put his ass on Cottage!"

"Hello, Nathan working hard today?" Sandra said smiling.

"Hard as hell, why don't yall get some professionals out here to do some of this shit?"

"Watch your mouth! This is a church! Show some dignity," she said sternly.

"What if I told you I'd rather watch you?"

"I'd tell you to concentrate on that wall, something you can handle," she said with a sly smirk as she walked away.

Nate sat in amazement that he had been shot down.

"And a swing and a miss, ladies and gentlemen," I said mocking him.

"She digs me, I can tell. Just need a little time, that's all, you'll see," Nate said confidently.

I was happy that he was settling down enough to at least take an interest in a woman, it had been close to a year since the death of Gabby, and the baby and Nate was starting to come to grips with their loss. He seemed to be in a good mood, so I figured I would talk a little about the future.

"You know, Nate, we got about a million dollars stashed away, after this, maybe we should quietly move to Canada or Mexico."

"Yeah, I was thinking about that. But not until I find out who killed my family, I ain't letting that shit go, G."

I didn't press the matter, he was making progress, an argument might set him back, and neither I nor Rev. Fisher wanted that."

After about four months, Deacon Jackson started to talk more to Nate and I, he started by inviting us to an evening service held at a church in Chicago.

"Rev Fisher asked me to invite you boys to our annual revival next week; you can ride out with the rest of us in the church bus. The service starts six in the evening but I'd like everyone to be ready by five fifteen." And with that, he closed the door to our room and walked away.

"He doesn't like us much, does he?" I asked Nate.

"I don't think so, but who cares? I ain't done nothing to him. To tell you the truth, I don't care for his ass either," Nate said with a chuckle.

As I sat down on the firm mattress, I picked up the remote for the new television set Nate and I bought. That old black and white was just not going to do it! I turned the channel to seven; I always had the hots for Mary Ann Childers! I turned it on just in time to see her go into the story about Jon. The jury found him guilty on all counts and he was handed down two consecutive life terms for his "crimes against humanity" as the judge termed it. When they showed a picture of him, he seemed to have gained some weight, but still looked hollow.

"Damn, they stuck it to him, didn't they?" Nate said.

"Yeah, it all seems so unfair, though; everybody being dead and Jon going to jail for the rest of his life while we get a second shot at it, doesn't seem right."

"Well like the Rev. said, maybe God likes us," Nate said smiling.

"That isn't what he has been teaching us, he said God is a God of justice, and this is not justice Nate."

"Man, what is it with you? You're like the grim reaper or something! When shit is going good I can always count on you for some negative shit! I'm going downstairs."

As he stormed out of the door, I sat down to try and figure out how I could find out what prison Jon was being sent to and ponder on ways to set up communication with him. I just felt bad about it all. I needed to talk to someone, and I knew just who I could trust.

"See G, that motherfucker sold that whole kilo in about a week. He's a natural I told you," he said slapping me on the back and boasting. He always liked to be right.

"Maybe, and maybe it's just that we have good stuff, maybe that area you gave him is a hot area, which it is. Maybe the shit sold itself, maybe anyone you put in that area would have had the same success."

"You live to contradict me, don't you, boy? Well, he made his money, now he gotta make some for us! I'm putting his ass back out there!"

"Why Nate? The guy wants out! You are right. He made his money, now let him go."

"Fuck you, this ain't no damn charity shit, this is a business! That motherfucker paid on his principle, now he gotta pay us some interest! It's the American way," he said smiling.

"Nate, this guy has a family, you keep putting him out there and something bad is going to happen. Besides, he ain't gonna go back out there anyway," I reasoned.

"He ain't got no choice, G, what the fuck you think, I'm gonna give him an option? You know how I work. Tell Dana to put his fucking ass back out there, and if he refuses, buck his ass!"

"Nate, he's gonna run to the police and you know that."

"Then I'll kill his wife and kids, now somebody's either going to work or the morgue, it's up to him. I don't give a shit."

"Rev Fisher, can I talk to you for a moment?"

"Sure son, but let's talk outside, I got some gardening to do if you don't mind or do you prefer the office?"

"It's ok, I need some air anyway."

As he slipped on his work shoes and put on his baseball cap, I marveled at how simple and happy a man he was. He seemed so at peace with himself and his life. There was a bit of humidity in the air and I could still feel the freshness of spring in the atmosphere. He had been working on his garden for about three years; to say he had a green thumb would be a lie. As the passersby gave him the usual "hello Reverend and how do you do", I felt so out of place. This was a world I was not used to, but I looked forward to becoming a part of it. Living my life with a spirit of simplicity, not having to look over my shoulder at every turn, God how I wanted that!

As we walked around the back of the church, Rev. Fisher stood with his hands on his hips and surveyed the lot.

"You know, Derrick, God has blessed us all with many gifts, but a man must know his limitations," he said with a smile referring to his mess of a garden.

"Oh Rev. Fisher, you will get it there, you'll see."

"Nah, I don't think so. You know if I could just get one of these flowers to bud, I think I would be ok," he said with a smile. As he unraveled the huge cord for his power tools, he turned his attention to me.

"What's troubling you, son?"

"Oh boy, where do I begin?" I said as I let out a deep sigh.

"I just found out that one of our friends received a large prison sentence for his involvement in what we were into, and it's gotten me down."

"Jonathan Mullenrand, I heard about that."

"How did you connect him with us?"

"Wasn't hard son, you and Nathan have not been very open about the details concerning your drug dealing, so I did my homework. And with the help of the Holy Spirit I was able to connect the dots, so to speak."

I dropped my head in shame. I didn't know what to say, we were basically fugitives at this church, and up until now we thought we had the Reverend fooled.

"Hand me that rake, son. You know, Derrick, you and Nathan have done horrible things, I understand how you feel. Maybe you should have turned yourselves in and cooperated with the authorities to help bring that man down, huh?"

He still didn't completely understand. He had been so nice to us, and really was putting himself and the church on the line by helping us. Plus, I felt the incredible need to confess, I was hurt, embarrassed, and ashamed so I let him have it, I told him everything;

The fact was Nathan and I were the real masterminds behind the operation, the people we had killed and destroyed because of our drug dealing. I was so overcome with emotion that I started to cry uncontrollably. I told him how I felt I let my mother down, and how much I missed her. I let out so much emotion that I thought I would scare him.

"It is just that you are suffering son, your sins are terrible. The Good news is you have someone that has paid the price for your sins. Jesus is waiting at the door of your heart son, let him in, and give your heart to Christ that you may have peace."

"I don't know, Rev. Fisher, I feel that I am beyond redemption, I don't think Jesus has the heart to forgive someone like me." I said in between sobs.

"You are so wrong, Derrick, Jesus paid a tremendous price for you just for this moment."

"What do I say to Jesus? I don't know where to start."

"Tell him what you just told me, and invite him into your heart, right now, Derrick, before the Devil changes your mind. I will pray with you, come on."

Then I was ready, I got down on my knees and let it all out to God, I told him how rotten I had been. I told him how helpless I felt and how I wanted him to change my heart. I couldn't believe I was on my knees outside in the open for everyone to see me praying, but I didn't care. The burden of my sins became too much to bear. After I prayed, I got up and gave Rev. Fisher a hug and I looked at him and noticed that he had been crying.

"What are you crying for?"

"It is very emotional to me for a soul to come to Christ, and it is a time for celebration." He said wiping his face and adjusting his cap back on his bald head.

"Rev. Fisher, I don't think I will be a good Christian but I can do my best."

"Nonsense, you will be a great soldier for Christ, you will see."

I felt so free, I felt like everything would be ok. I didn't realize how despondent I had felt ever since I found my mother dead many years ago. I felt I had a new beginning in life, and I wanted so desperately not to let God or Rev. Fisher down. Now I had to tell Nate, I couldn't wait to see and hear his reaction.

Chapter 4

"I'll be damned, they done turned you out too, huh?" Nate said mockingly.

"It's not like that, Nate; I really gave my heart to Christ today," I said in defense.

"That's good, G, but don't try and pull that goody goody shit with me, I'm keeping shit real."

"So am I. God is real, Nate, and you should give him a try also. Rev. Fisher told me that-

"Aww shit now here you go! Just because he brainwashed you with that shit, don't try and fry my head with it, leave me alone," he said in a huff.

"Never mind, I must have been crazy to think you would listen."

As I finished my sentence Sandra knocked on our door.

"Dinner will be served in about an hour, sister Jackson fell ill so I am filling in for her, hope you enjoy what I have made," she said smiling.

"Oh boy! This is great, you gon' kill me, and G can put me in heaven tonight," Nate said joking.

"Yes, congratulations, Derrick, I heard about your conversion today. Welcome to God's family," she said opening her arms for a hug.

"Can I get a hug too?" Nate asked smiling.

"Get saved and I will hug you also."

"So I gotta join a cult to get a hug?"

Sandra simply rolled her eyes and walked out of the room.

Nate was trying in his own way to be liked, but he was going about it the wrong way. He didn't understand that he was completely insulting everyone by mocking what they believed in. Everyone was tolerating Nate for the sake of Rev. Fisher, but their tolerance level was beginning to wear thin.

"Nate, you gotta give everyone a break, you can't just rip what people believe in, it's insulting and it hurts people."

"Yeah whatever. Look, I think I know where they are sending Jon."

"Where?"

"Georgia State Penitentiary, it's maximum security, it's just outside some town called Reidsville, think I wanna write him a letter, what do you think?"

"I think it's a bad idea, you don't want to open communication with Jon, he might flip and turn us in. The last thing he probably wants to hear is that we are on the outside getting a second chance while he is looking at life in prison! Let him alone Nate."

"I ain't contacting him for no small talk, G, he might know who killed my family that's what I wanna talk about!"

"Nate, if you send him a letter that will lead the police straight to us. Use your head."

"Not me fool, I was thinking of getting one of these motherfuckers around here to do it, you know disguise it as a prison ministry or some shit."

I just looked at him and walked out of the room. Getting closer to God allowed me to begin to see just how sick Nate really was.

****

"Hey Nate it's me, Dana."

"What's up baby?"

"I got Al's wife out here, you know the lame we gave the kilo to about a month ago."

"Fuck does she want?"

"I don't know she won't talk or tell, but she says it's important."

Nate motioned to let her in. As she walked into the massive office, Dana stopped her at the door and began to frisk her for any weapons.

"What's your name, babe?"

"Uh, my name is Latonia, I am Al's wife and I wanted to talk to you. Are you Nate?" she asked sheepishly.

"What do you need to talk to me about?" Nate said ignoring the question.

The woman gave a quick look at Dana as if to say she wanted this meeting to be private.

"That's my bodyguard, she stays, now talk."

The young woman adjusted herself to sit down and asked if she could have a drink.

"Look girl, I ain't got time for socializing, talk or get the fuck out!"

Clearly intimidated and afraid, she began her petition.

"I heard you are a reasonable man and if something makes sense you would listen and consider. Well, my husband is really having a tough time out there and he wants to stop doing this. Last night, he came home beat up by someone and it scared me and the children. This isn't the life that he is used to, he originally came to you because my middle child had a terrible infection and her medical bills were too much for us. I wasn't working at the time, so he did what he had to do, you understand? But now this life is destroying us and we really need to move on, we can't handle it."

Nate listened intently and reached for a cigar from the beautiful box, clipped the end of it, and lit it.

"Dana, give her a drink. What are you drinking, sweetie?"

"Rum and Coke."

"That's good, Rum and Coke, Dana, you know I understand your situation and I sympathize with you, but I am a businessman, and your husband was fronted a large amount of powder, which he has neither sold nor returned, I mean that's not good."

"We still have it at home; I mean I could get it back to you. That's not a problem."

"Ok, tell you what, honey, finish your drink and you go back home and get that stuff I'll have one of my guys escort you there and bring you back so you will be safe. And while you are gone, I will think about a way we can handle this."

As the young woman got up to get her drink from Dana, Nate surveyed her body with lust as he seemed to undress her with his thoughts and eyes.

"I knew you would understand, thank you for helping us out, Nate."

"No problem. I will see you this evening about eight?"

"That's fine, I will be here."

"Cool, uh hey why didn't Al come and talk to me?"

"He was nervous and he didn't want you to know that he had gotten beat up."

"I see. Dana, can I see you outside for a minute?"

As Dana and Nate walked outside the office the young woman, now more relaxed surveyed the immense office and marveled at what drug money could actually buy.

"You trust her?" Dana asked.

"Yeah, I knew this bitch from Robeson back in the day, and I know her family, she all good. She got a fat ass though!" Nate said lustfully.

"What do you want me to do?"

"See to it that she gets back here with the stuff this evening alone. Her punk ass husband sent her here to do what he should have been doing! I hate a bitch ass man!"

"Yeah, no shit! I was thinking that too," Dana said

"Well get her back here tonight, oh and make sure G aint here, ok?"

"Cool."

Nate and I had helped to basically rehab the entire church, and I was pretty proud of our work. The Deacons had shown Nate and I how to paint, hang drywall, and lay ceramic tile, it was great. Nate seemed to enjoy working and talking, something we had not done since the McDonald's days. He was starting to open up more, and talk about the future, and less about finding Gabby and baby Glo's killers. I guess he resided within himself that it wasn't going to happen. It took Nate about three months to finally talk freely about missing them and less about revenge. I noticed he was starting to take steps toward closure, and that was huge for him.

"You know, G, I been thinking about getting a tattoo, you know of Gabby and Glo on my arm. What do you think?"

"I think it's cool Nate, but what if you get married again?"

"Shit, I don't care, the next broad I marry will have to accept it. I loved them, I know they are gone but I still think about them a lot."

"That's understandable. Hey, you still trying your hand with Sandra?"

"Yeah, gonna have to break that one down bit by bit. Don't think the Rev. is too keen on it though."

"What makes you say that?"

"Well me and him were painting and he asked me about her, and if I was interested. I told him kind of, and he goes: well she is a woman of God Nate, you must treat her as such."

"Well that's true, Nate, she's a good girl you know."

Just as I finished my sentence I noticed a knock at the church door, which made no sense because everyone in the community knew the church was always open to the public, who would knock? I stole a look from the side window before going in to open it and it was the guy who was taking pictures from the car months ago.

"Nate, it's him! It's the guy with the camera I was telling you about!"
Nate peered through the window and squinted as to concentrate on his appearance.
"Never seen him before, what should we do?"
"No one else is here, let's just not answer it."
"Yeah, but what if it's important? The Rev. has a lot of important people looking for him."
"Don't answer it, Nate, it could be trouble."
The young man stood back from the door and started looking through the windows hoping to see someone, but the window's were stained glass and tough to see anyone from inside the church, and impossible to see in from outside.
"Fuck! What does he want?"
"Nate, watch your mouth. Ok he's walking away, maybe he's gonna leave."
The man sat in the car and pulled out a pad and began to write as he glanced up to the church seemingly in-between sentences as he wrote. After about five minutes he threw the pad in the passenger side seat and drove away.
"See, I told you it's crazy, don't you think?"
"Yeah, I don't know, G, maybe we should blow this place. We stick around here and we may get found."
"Nate, we can't just leave, Rev. Fisher went to a lot of trouble for us, that wouldn't be right."
"So what, stay here and go to jail? Fuck that!"
"You know now that we are on the subject, is there something you need to tell me? I've been asking you for six months about a third party that may have been involved and you keep side-stepping the question, what's up?"
"Nothing, there was no one involved, G, it was always just us."

"Back in those days you and Jon would always go out to meetings once every three months or so and be gone for hours, who were you meeting with?"

"G, would you quit! Just meetings with other gangsters about turf shit, that's all."

Then the phone rang, Nate picked it up after the first ring, again trying to avoid the subject.

"The good Rev. says he is on his way it's time for our bible study are we done here?"

"Yeah, Nate, for now."

I must admit there was a part of me that wanted to know, and another part of me that did not, sometime ignorance truly is bliss.

After our bible study later that night, Rev. Fisher asked us about going to the evening service the upcoming Sunday.

"Do we have to?" Nate asked.

"Nathan, you don't have to do anything, but I would be disappointed if you didn't. It's a very spiritual service and promises to be a great time with the Lord; I think you boys would enjoy it."

"I'd rather stay here and paint," Nate lamented under his breath.

"We will be there Reverend, and we look forward to it," I spoke up.

"Then it is settled, you two will ride to the church with us and we will eat shortly thereafter," Rev. Fisher said with glee, as Nate stared out of the window with regret.

****

"Ok, Nate she back, you want me to bring her in?" Dana asked

"Yeah, G is gone, right?"

"Yeah, he left with big Mike to see a movie they gonna be gone for a while."

"Good, bring her in, but frisk her ass good, first."

After frisking her, Dana showed her once again into the massive office, while Nate stood at the fireplace and tended to the fire.

"Did you bring the stuff?" Nate asked without looking around as he poked at the logs in the fire.

"Yes, one kilo as agreed," she said tentatively.

"What kind of cut?"

"You gave it to us with a one, and I think he cut it once more."

Nate slid the poker in the holder and walked away from the fire. He grabbed the cellophane bag and opened it. He pulled a switch blade from his pocket and stuck it in the bag to grab some with the tip of the blade.

"Looks like my shit, but you know the real test is in the high," as he held it up to the woman's nose for her to snort. She stood there for a second deciding whether or not she should snort. As she leaned in for the hit, Nate gently eased the tip of the blade to her left nostril, and she took in a big sniff. Nate gave a slight smile, dipped the blade for the other nostril, and once again the woman took in a huge sniff. The woman stood there for a moment and walked carefully over to the plush leather sofa and plopped down on it, clearly giving away the fact that this was her first high.

"Yeah, that's my shit!" Nate said loudly with devilish laughter.

Dana nodded and smiled with approval.

"Give this girl a drink Dana, I like her!" Nate said with a wide smile.

"Rum and Coke please," she said wiping her nose slowly with careful intent.

Nate wrapped the bag of cocaine slowly and tossed it across the room at Dana.

"You know, I think I know you. Did you graduate from Robeson high?"

"Yeah, class of eighty-seven."

"Bingo! I told you I knew her Dana," Nate said winking his eye.

Nate sat down in his high back leather chair behind the large wooden desk, and lit another cigar as he accepted a drink of Cognac from Dana. Once Nate saw the woman was clearly high, he began his ruse.

"You know, I hate to disappoint a home girl, but I gotta keep yall in this shit," he said plainly.

"But Nate, you promised-"

"Hey wait dammit, I didn't promise you shit! I told you I would think about it."

"Don't you see we can't? Don't you see this is destroying our family why are you doing this to us?" The woman said starting to cry.

Frankly, because your hubby is good at selling it," Nate said without remorse.

The woman began to sob childishly. Nate tossed her a box of Kleenex, leaned back in his and propped his feet up on the corner of the desk.

"Ok, ok tell you what I will do. Just to show that I am a kindhearted guy, I will put your husband back out there for six months and then I will pull him and call it even Steven on one condition."

The woman looked up from her tissue with a glimmer of hope on her face.

"That I can get a little ass from you from time to time, I think you're a fine ass bitch, and I wouldn't mind tapping that ass a little while you make that money," Nate said with a sly grin.

"No!" the young woman said with sincerity.

"Fuck you then! Dana, put this nigga on the street and pull him when I say so!" Nate said angrily.

"No! He will die out there, Nate, you know that!"

Nate didn't look up as he pulled a large ledger from his desk and ignored her. Dana pulled out her phone and began to make a call to the appropriate people to put the man on the street.

"Nate, please don't make me do this! Ok, I tell you what we will sell it at a seventy thirty split," the woman said trying to make an alternative deal.

Nate never looked up as he flipped through the pages seemingly unconcerned with her attempts at renegotiating. Dana finally reached the appropriate people and started to give the woman's address.

"How can you do this to a mother, Nate?" The woman said with eyes full of tears.

Nate took a large drag from his cigar and flipped another page of the large ledger.

The woman dropped her head and inwardly resigned her fate.

"Ok, you win I will do it only for my family," she said in-between sobs.

"Frankly, I don't give a fuck who you do it for, but that's a good girl," Nate said as he motioned for Dana to end the call.

The woman started toward the door and Nate stopped her.

"Uh this deal begins tonight," Nate said with a sneer.

The woman's eyes widened as she could not believe his complete lack of compassion. She slowly walked toward the desk with visible shame and disgust. As she approached the desk, she gave a look at Dana once again.

"That's my bodyguard, she stays," Nate said with a grin.

As the woman began to cry once again, she slowly undid her jeans.

"Nah, just a little head tonight is cool," Nate said placing his hand over hers.

The woman felt completely helpless; emotions engulfed her as she started to cry uncontrollably. Nate turned toward her and stood, unzipped his pants and sat back down. As Dana stood at the door nodding in criminal approval, her smile soon turned to sadness, as memories of her and her sisters sexual abuse came to life. She turned quietly and walked out of the door as Nate laid his head back in the chair with pleasure, no need to watch as another woman is exploited and demeaned by a man for sex.

CHAPTER 5

As Nate and I got ready for the trip to the evening service, I could tell that he had something he wanted to talk about. Usually he would get extremely fidgety and pace uncontrollably. Depending on what it was, I would either convince him to talk, or ignore his actions until I was ready to take on what he needed to talk about. That night, neither would take place.

"You know, G, I am really tired of this damp cold ass room!"

"Beats a jail cell!"

He glared at me and continued to fidget with his necktie, then a knock at our room door.

"You boys need to be downstairs by six-thirty, the bus leaves at quarter till, and the service starts at seven-thirty," Deacon Jackson said with his husky voice through the closed door.

"You can come in Deacon," I said.

The door eased slightly open with its usual creaking sound. Jackson peered into the room and gave a quick panoramic scan of our quarters.

"As I said, the bus leaves at-"

"We heard you homeboy, no need to repeat all of that again," Nate said agitated.

"Mind your tone, young man, I am your elder! You need to learn some manners!"

"Hey man, fuck you, who do you think you are coming into our room talking shit-"

"Hey Nate, cool it man!"

I could see things were getting out of hand because Deacon Jackson completely entered the room and slammed the door behind him.

"I know you come from the streets boy, but in case you didn't know it, you are no longer there! But that is exactly where I am gonna send you, I don't care if it hair lips the pastor!" Jackson said with his southern accented deep voice. Just as Nate was about to explode, Sandra knocked at the door, and announced that she was coming in.

"What is going on in here? I can hear you all from downstairs!"

"Hey Sandra, tell this black motherfucker to go kick some rocks with his country ass and step off before I-"

Sandra gave Nate a look I had not seen since momma Williams was alive.

"Everyone leave this room and give Nathan and I a word alone right now!" she said through gritted teeth.

Deacon Jackson flung the door open and stormed out of the room visibly seething and I followed, wishing I could stay and hear what was about to happen.

Once everyone had left, Sandra walked toward Nate as his eyes widened revealing his uneasiness of the situation.

"We have all bent over backward for you since you have been here; we have waited on you, hand and foot, accommodated your every whim and desire. But I will not allow you to disrespect my father that way! He is a good man, and despite his personal feelings toward you, he has been nice to you, now you owe him an apology, and if you don't, well, you can just forget you and I ever being more than just incidental associates!" Nate fell for her right there! He always had a thing for strong outspoken women. But she was right, Nate had been acting like a real asshole around here, but what really threw him for a loop was to find out that Deacon Jackson was Sandra's father! That one blew him away. Now, he had to watch how he treated and talked to the old guy. Quiet as it was kept, Nate liked Sandra, and didn't want to upset her. He actually cared what she thought of him and wanted to give a good impression. For the rest of the day, he was pretty quiet until we boarded the bus to go to the church service.

"Hey G, I really fucked up dude, I didn't know the old man was her father."

"Don't worry about it, Nate, it's done now just watch what you say to him man. You gotta be nicer to these people, man, they are trying to help us and they are really nice people."

"I know, dude, just really under a lot of stress."

That was an understatement; Nate was having a lot of bad dreams lately, and keeping me up most nights, he had been complaining of headaches, and he seemed very paranoid. I guess the stress of a life lived selling drugs and ruining lives was starting to catch him.

When we arrived at the church, Rev Fisher came to Nate and I to tell how things would go. It turns out that many of the local pastors had heard of Fisher's little ministry of helping Nate and I. He was so proud of that, especially since things seemed to be working out fairly well. We walked into the vestibule of the church, and I immediately noticed how great it smelled in there. I noticed that the women had been burning potpourri, and there were fresh flowers everywhere. There were scriptures framed that adorned the walls, along with pictures of Dr. King and scenes from the civil rights movement. When I opened the French doors that led into the sanctuary, it was beautiful; there was a burgundy color scheme to the pews and carpet. Wood pulpit furniture aligned across the front of the church and the stained glass windows added a sense of serenity. I stood at the doors with my mouth open until I was interrupted by Nate.

"Pretty fancy place, huh?"

"Yeah really nice, puts our place to shame," I said

"Well that ain't real hard to do," Nate said sarcastically.

"What do you think, boys?" Rev. Fisher asked.

"Really nice Rev. Fisher, never been in a church this nice before."

"How do they clean these ceilings, they are so high?" I asked.

Rev. Fisher smiled and walked us toward the pastor of the church.

"Derrick, Nate, this is Rev. Thompson. He is the pastor of the church. Carl, these are the boys I told you about."

"Good to meet you boys, welcome to Mt. Sinai, it is a pleasure to meet you both."

Rev. Thompson was a tall man with salt and pepper hair and a wide smile. He seemed to be near Rev. Fisher's age. We walked to his office and discussed how good God is and how our lives had changed. After small talk and a great meal, it was time to begin the service. Today was supposed to be a special service for "sinners" and Rev. Fisher wanted Nate to pay special attention to the sermon, so he instructed me to sit further toward the front of the church away from Nate. We all received a pamphlet with the order of service; and it was time to begin. The service began the way most do in the traditional black Baptist church; there was a devotional where the Deacons chanted what is called a "Dr. Watts", the choir processional, scripture readings, alter prayer, choir selections, and then the "Good News."

From time to time during the service, I would peek back at Nate to make sure he was paying attention and not asleep as he had done through many of these services. But I noticed this time that Rev. Fisher had stationed Sandra right next to him! The sermon was actually pretty good; Rev. Fisher's title was called "Divine Appointment". He went on to tell us that death was a divine appointment that we all had to keep, and that we should be ready for the hereafter. Rev.

Fisher was a very good speaker, and seemed to hold everyone's attention. The thing I liked about his sermons the most was that they were never really long. After his sermon, Rev. Fisher "opened the door to Christ" this is where a sinner would publicly come up front to receive Christ as their personal savior. I peeked back once again to see Sandra whispering something into Nate's ear, I saw Nate purse his lips together and nod no. I knew Nate was not ready, everyone there seemed to want so badly for him to come, but I remember Rev. Fisher once said it is a personal choice, and only when the time and the spirit is right will the person make the choice.

After the service we all stood around in the sanctuary small talking and I saw Nate sitting in the back of the church in the last pew alone. I started toward him and Rev. Fisher tugged at my arm.

"Let him alone, the Holy Spirit is dealing with him right now. His time is coming, I can feel it." He went on to talk about what he called "spiritual warfare," where the good in us battled the bad in us for control. He explained that is what Nate was going through. He went on to tell me that Nate had changed tremendously from who he was at the hospital, and how the whole congregation was praying for him. As we all started to walk outside, I saw a man sitting in a car parked across the street looking at the church. Before I completely walked out, I jerked myself back in not to be seen by him. He looked as if he was waiting for someone, so I waited to see if any of the parishioners would get into the car with him. After ten minutes, no one walked toward the car, I started to get nervous. I went to get Nate.

"Hey, we got a problem," I whispered to him.

"What is it?"

"There's a guy parked across the street looking at the church, just sitting there."

"Maybe he is a ride for somebody."

"No, that's what I thought, but nobody is going toward him
or getting in."

"Shit!"

"Should we tell Rev. Fisher?"

"No, I noticed another exit near the choir stand let's just
ease out that way," Nate said.

I was getting so tired of living this way; sneaking around
and hiding. It was really getting old, but what could we do?
We had made our beds; maybe this was our penalty for a
life of sin. I was so confused.

****

"Nate there's something I want to talk to you about."

"Come on in, brother, how is shit going out there? Money
is coming in great baby! We rolling like Kid and Play
nigga!" Nate said with glee.

"We got a problem."

"What is it? Spill it nigga!"

"Al is gone."

"Fuck you mean gone? Did you go by his house?"

"We just left there, we kicked in the door of the house and
all of the furniture and shit is gone. I think they moved or
something."

Nate looked down at his desk and swirled his cigar
around in his mouth as he knocked on his desk.

"How much is he in to us for."

"Well, we did find a kilo of coke on the bedroom floor but
all the money is gone."

"How much?"

Mike didn't want to tell Nate, fearing his reaction so, he
stalled and looked down at the floor.

"How much, motherfucker?!" Nate yelled.

"Close to 300 hundred grand Nate, but-"

"But my ass nigga, he was your responsibility! Now get your fat ass outta here and bring me Dana!" Nate screamed.

Nate slammed his ledger book closed and began to pace and think, folding his powerfully built arms and blowing cigar smoke until Dana walked in.

"What's up, Nate?"

"This motherfucker let Al and his family walk away with 300 thousand of my fucking money! Now I want you to find his ass, Dana, and I don't care what you have to do, or who you have to kill to do it! You understand?"

"I gotcha."

Nate motioned for her to leave the room; after she left, he threw a glass of Cognac into the fireplace enraged.

****

Nate expressed interest in Sandra from the first time he met her at the hospital, he was impressed with her. When she spoke to him forcefully about her father, that seemed to have sparked even more interest. Besides, she seemed too interested, and cared very much about his future and his salvation. He realized he had offended her terribly, and wanted to make amends.

"Hey Sandra, can I speak to you a moment?" Nate asked sheepishly.

"Sure."

"Uh, I don't exactly know how to say this but…..I am sorry about what I said about your father. I honestly didn't know that he was your father, if I knew that I-"

"Should it make a difference, Nathan? He is an older man, and should be treated with respect. His being my father is inconsequential."

"It's what?"

"Never mind, I accept your apology," she said dryly continuing her tiding up of the church kitchen.

Nate fidgeted a while and spoke again.

"You know I saw this cute little café on our way home from the service last night, maybe I can take you there for a cup of coffee or something, you know to try and make amends."

"Really?" Sandra said smiling.

"Well, yeah. I like coffee and I know you do too, I thought it would be a good chance for us to get to know each other."

"I don't know if that is a good idea, Nathan."

"You can call me Nate."

"I prefer Nathan if it's ok with you."

"Why can't you have coffee with me, and why can't we get to know each other?"

"Because I don't know if we have anything in common."

"Well girl, that's why I want to get to know you. What are you afraid of?"

"I'm not afraid of anything, Nathan, I just like a different type of man, that's all."

"Sandra, let's just go have coffee please."

"I'll think about it and let you know tomorrow."

Nate felt it was pointless, what was there to think about? He felt she was interested in him and just playing hard to get.

"G, I tell you the chick is playing games, she just wants me to chase her."

"Nate, you gotta look at it from her point of view. She really doesn't know you that well."

"You and her live in the same world of confusion, that's why I want to get to know her!"

"Ok Nate, let's put it this way, she doesn't really know you, and she doesn't know if she wants to get to know you."

"Why not?"

He just wasn't getting it, so I told him to take it slow and be more understanding. Things were going pretty well, we were both learning the bible, and getting to know the people there pretty well. Nate was softening up and spent a lot of time reading and talking to Sandra. Rev. Fisher announced a going-away celebration for his son Jeremiah; he was going to study at a seminary down south. I knew Rev. Fisher would miss him, they were really close. Deacon Jackson and Nate made-up, and were talking about painting the ceiling of the church together. But Nate talked more about his coffee date with Sandra. He was really looking forward to it. After bugging me to death about what he should wear and all, they finally got together in the church vestibule to go out.

"You look nice, and I love your eyes," Nate said smiling.

"Thank you, you look nice also."

Being afraid of the "man in the car," Nate asked Sandra if she would drive and she agreed.

Nate was the perfect gentleman; he put on her jacket for her, opened the car doors and even pulled out her chair for her at the café. Unlike the Nate I know.

"So, I finally got you here," Nate said smiling.

"Yeah, this is a nice little place, Nathan, real quiet."

"I know."

Nate placed his elbows on the table and leaned forward and gave a romantic look at Sandra.

"Tell me something, how is it that a woman as cute as you is not married with children?"

"I was married once."

"Really, what happened?"

"He was a great man, we had a wonderful marriage. I was very in love with him, Nathan. We were trying to have children, but we had trouble. A doctor told me I could not have children. Then he was killed in a drive by shooting. Rival gang bangers shooting and vying for drug turf."

Knowing his past, he figured that he should not travel down that area.

"I'm really sorry about that Sandra. Maybe you will meet another great guy."

"If it is God's will, I am hopeful. Tell me about your wife and daughter."

"Well, I loved them dearly too. Losing them broke my heart, I feel responsible because of the life I lived. I try not to think too hard about it, cause it gets me down," Nate said reaching into his pocket for a picture to show Sandra.

"They are beautiful, Nathan, I am sorry also," she said handing back the picture to him.

"See, we do have something in common," Nate said smiling.

"Yeah, I guess we do."

"Sandra, I know I am from the street, and I know what I was, but I am trying to change. I wish people would just give me a chance."

"Everyone is, Nathan, it takes time."

"Your father is not, he doesn't really know me, but he hates me, why?"

"He doesn't hate you, Nathan. My father has been through a lot. Losing my mother years ago and the situation with my brother has taken its toll on him."

"What's up with your brother?"

"I'd rather not say."

Understanding her pain, Nate received his coffee from the waitress and started to take a sip.

"Nathan, may I ask you a question?"

"Sure."

"Have you ever killed a man before?"

"I'd rather not say," Nate said looking out of the café's window in deep reflection.

****

CHAPTER 6

"Nate, I was going over the accounts yesterday and it looks like your guy Al got away with about 287,000 bucks," Jon said

"Yeah, and it's all Mike's fault! I told that motherfucker to keep an eye on his ass, and then this cocksucker and his family disappear under his watch like a fucking fart in the wind!" Nate said angrily.

Then Dana walked in smiling with what Nate would call good news.

"We still haven't found him, but we got a cousin downstairs and her little son."

"Is she talking?"

"Nah, I slapped her around a bit, but she still says she doesn't know anything."

"Bullshit, I bet I can get her to talk!" Nate said rising up out of his chair.

Nate led Dana and some of her ruthless staff of mafia guys through the underground tunnel that led to what Nate called the "terror chamber." This was where they would murder and torture people when needed. The closer they came to the chamber the more rotten the smell became. Some of the most ruthless murders imaginable were committed here and old blood and rotten flesh began to emanate and blend into the air.

Nate opened the heavy steel door, took off his shirt and walked toward the woman now nearly white with fear. She was bound and gagged along with her son sitting near back to back. Nate snatched off the gag and began his interrogation.

"Look bitch, I ain't fucking with you. Now I wanna know where your boy Al and his family went with my money. He stole three hundred grand from me and I am gonna get it! Now where the fuck is he?" Nate growled.

"I told her, I don't know, we saw Al a week ago and he complained about how he was going through some things, and that was it. We really ain't that close so he wouldn't tell me anything like that. Please let my son and I go, we won't say anything, I swear! We just want to go back to our lives!" The woman said trembling in fear.

Nate looked at her and gave a half smile, then moved close to her ear as to not let anyone hear what he was saying.

"Look bitch, don't fuck with me. I will pull my dick out and make you suck it right here in front of this punk ass boy of yours! Then I'm gonna let these boys around here ass rape your son until you talk, and maybe after his ass is bleeding for a while you might want to tell me something, huh?"

The woman looked at Nate as if she had seen the devil.

"Oh my God no, please don't do that! I told you everything I know, I swear, please don't hurt my son! He is all I have," the woman said crying uncontrollably.

Nate grabbed her by her hair and began to scream.

"Then talk bitch!"

"My God, Jesus I don't know anything, I swear!" The woman balled out like a baby.

Nate walked toward Dana and started toward the huge steel door again.

"Get me some info, and be creative ok! Stop paddy caking with this bitch!" Nate snarled as he walked out of the door.

****

"You know, Deacon Jackson, I am sorry about the other day, I'm just under a lot of pressure," Nate said apologetically.

"It's ok, boy, just remember we are all trying to help you. But you have to know that things are different here in the world, you just can't act the same way you did as a drug dealer."

Nate was once again offended, but bit his tongue, if for nothing but for Sandra's sake.

"Now let's discuss how we gonna paint that ceiling tomorrow, my friend is gonna be here early in the morning to help us build a scaffold. I need you to be up at seven a.m," Deacon Jackson said.

"Yeah, ok," Nate said dryly.

Rev. Fisher and I worked on Jeremiah's going-away celebration; I guess he felt it was a good idea to talk to me about things. He seemed to be more trusting with me as far as those things went.

"I've been really tired lately; think I need a check-up again. I asked God to keep me healthy until my boy finishes the seminary; I trust he will honor that," Fisher said reflecting.

I looked out of the window hearing him, but I was deep in thought myself.

"You know, Rev. Fisher, Nate said something to me last night that got me thinking."

"Yeah, and what was that?" Fisher said going through his rolodex.

"He said he was not going to live."

"Well he won't, none of us are," Fisher said smiling and flipping through the cards.

No, I mean he said he wasn't going to live long. I was teasing him about going out with Sandra. I said I would be there for their wedding and wanted to be an uncle to their children. I teased him about growing old and grey with

Sandra, you know silly stuff, and he said he wouldn't live to see fifty."

"Maybe he won't. Derrick, death is not the end, it is the beginning. You should not be too concerned with him dying but rather, you should worry about him possibly dying in his sins."

I really didn't care about that at all, Nate was all the family I had in the world and the thought of him dying and me being left alone was too scary of a thought. Yet I knew we had done so much, how could he or I live long?

Later that night, I decided to talk to Nate about it, to see what he meant.

"Hey Nate, what did you mean when you said earlier that you wouldn't live to see fifty?"

"G, you are one of the most serious guys I know," Nate said laughing.

"Nah, just wondering, you know you are my brother. Don't want you going nowhere," I said trying to lighten the conversation.

"The future is what it is G, we can't control it. Ain't that what yall say around here, it's all in God's hands?" Nate said sarcastically.

I shrugged my shoulders, said my prayers, and climbed into bed. I peeked over at Nate to find him reading his bible and reading a book Sandra gave him called "The power of Prayer". I thought "wow," if Dana and Mike could only see him now.

■■■

It was getting late, and Nate started to wonder how Dana's interrogation was going, he wrapped about four hundred grand in plastic and stuck it into the wall safe. He washed his hands and headed down the steps to the underground tunnel leading to the dreaded area. During the walk, he lit a cigar and rubbed his muscled arms and hoped

Dana had something for him. He walked into the room, and walked immediately to Dana for his report.

"Ok, talk to me."

"Man, she don't know shit," Dana resigned.

"You sure?" Nate asked.

"Dude, we been raping and beating this bitch for hours, a couple of the mafia guys even beat the shit out of her son right in front of her. She's a tough broad, started mumbling some shit right before she passed out," Dana said

"What about the boy, he know anything?"

"Shit, Nate, he's dead."

Nate walked over to the woman's beaten, and bloody naked body and lifted her head up by her hair and looked at her face. The woman seemed to be passed out, obviously grief stricken and in shock.

"Yeah, her goose is cooked. Give me your piece." He motioned to Dana for her gun.

Nate cocked the gun and blew the woman's brains out obviously putting her out of her misery.

"Ok clean all this shit up, and get rid of the bodies. You know what to do."

"What now, Nate?" Dana asked.

"Get me some more family members in here, somebody bound to know where this motherfucker is. We are not stopping until I get his ass in here with my money," Nate said walking out of the room.

****

Early the next morning, I woke up to find Nate already gone. I got washed up and dressed and came downstairs into the kitchen area to find mother Vincent.

"Good morning, mother Vincent, where is Nate?"

"Oh he's gone with Jackson to the hardware store, honey. They have been up for an hour or more. They're supposed to start the church ceiling this morning," she said with a smile.

I grabbed a glass of orange juice and headed toward the church sanctuary. I could see they had already set up the scaffold and had about thirty cans of paint spread around. As I surveyed the area, Rev. Fisher crept up behind me and scared me to death!

"No drinking in the sanctuary!" he said in a husky voice.

"Oh God you scared me! Good morning Rev. Fisher, where are you going so early?"

"Evangelism, son, there is more to being a pastor than standing up there and preaching," he said motioning up to the pulpit.

"Where do you go to do that?"

"Door to door, hey why don't you join me?"

"Well, Rev. I was gonna help mother Vincent in the kitchen area."

"She's fine, go get cleaned up. It will be a great experience for you."

I really didn't want to go; the idea of going door to door talking to people about God was a little scary. I knew people would probably slam doors in our faces, I liked my new life with God, but I don't know if I was quite cut out for that. Needless to say I got dressed and accompanied him in the church van to a very rough area on Joliet's west end. During the drive, Rev. Fisher kind of gave me a heads up on what to expect out there.

"It isn't gonna be pretty, Derrick, some people are gonna be pretty rude."

"Why can't we just talk to the ones that come to church on Sunday?"

"The church is God's house; that is the house of praise and worship. But Jesus expects us to go into the community, the world as a matter of fact and spread the good news," Rev. Fisher said proudly.

"If you say so."

"No Derrick, God said so."

After about twenty or thirty people completely ignoring us, one woman stopped to listen to Rev. Fisher.

"If you die tonight, ma'am, do you know where you would spend eternity?" Rev Fisher asked her.

"I don't know the woman said, but I am in a hurry right now. I have a court appearance for my son, could you pray for him, Reverend?" The watery eyed woman asked.

"Of course, but I am concerned about you right now, God wants your soul saved. Do you know the Lord?"

"Well I used to go to church when I was a girl, but that's been a long time ago," the woman said fastening her jacket.

"Pray with me the sinners prayer and give God your life, and then we will intercede on your son's behalf."

"I don't want my son to go to jail, Reverend."

The woman seemed more concerned with her son than her own soul, I think she would have said or done anything if it would save him. After praying with the woman and her giving her soul to Christ, Rev. Fisher gave her some Christian tracts with the church's information stamped on the back and she was on her way.

"What if she was not sincere?" I asked curiously.

"I really hope and pray she was, but if not, that is between her and the Lord. I try not to think about that. But many are sincere, Derrick, it is not our place to judge and try to speculate," he instructed.

We knocked on about thirty or forty more doors; we got some commitments from some to come to church on Sunday, and a couple to come to bible class. It was great to see Rev. Fisher in action, he really loved the gospel and loved talking about it and witnessing to others about God. He was warm and inviting, not pushy like some. Even if some people did not agree with him, they had to be nice to us, because Rev. Fisher was so nice. At about 1p.m. Rev. Fisher wanted to break for lunch.

"Well, what do you think about evangelizing, Derrick?"

"It seems tough, people can be really rude."

"Yeah they can be, but they don't know the Lord. What astounds me is when people claim they know God and are still rude and mean," he said smiling.

Sitting at a red light, Rev. Fisher's cell phone began to ring.

I noticed all of the people walking to and from seemingly in a hurry to go nowhere, children playing and the buying and selling of the various street merchants. It blew me away to think about what Rev. Fisher said to many people that day, that all of the people in the world would be judged by one God someday. That was awesome.

"We must get back to the church; it seems Nate was in an accident! He fell from the scaffold! Oh God please don't let anything be seriously wrong with him. Jesus please keep him," Rev. Fisher said with grief.

My heart was in my throat; all sorts of thoughts came to my head. My hands were sweaty, and I rocked back and forth in the front seat of that car.

"We are going straight to the hospital," Rev. Fisher said as he weaved thru the afternoon traffic.

I quietly closed my eyes and asked the Lord not to let him die, not to let anything be seriously wrong with him. I had prayed before in my brief new relationship with God, but not like this. My head was hurting with grief and worry as we pulled into the hospital parking lot. Deacon Jackson met us there in the emergency room with his friend; they still had their painting clothes on.

"I don't know, Reverend, he just slipped and fell. We tried to wake him up but he didn't respond so we called an ambulance. He wasn't that far up thank God," Jackson said obviously worried.

Sandra, mother Vincent and some other church members came rushing in with their faces flush with fear and concern.

"We all have to pray right now for him," Rev. Fisher said.

We all formed a circle and had a prayer for Nate. We all wanted to be strong and hopeful, but we were human, we were afraid for him.

Deacon Jackson paced a hole in that emergency room waiting area, surprisingly he was concerned and worried.

"Lord it's my fault. I knew he wasn't experienced, I should never have let him on that scaffold," he said as he wiped his teary face.

"Daddy, it's ok, Nathan will be ok. It wasn't your fault; God will bring him out better than new. I can feel it; God is working on him in there. Just him and the Holy Spirit, let God do his handiwork and let's all have faith," Sandra said convincingly.

I prayed she was right, I tried all I knew how to hold out faith, but it was tough.

After about an hour, the E.R nurse came over to talk to us. She told us Nate suffered a concussion and that he needed much rest, and that he would probably be under observation for a couple of days. Needless to say, we were all relieved and thanked God for answering our prayers. We went in two at a time to see him. He couldn't respond of course, he was pretty much out of it. When I saw him, he looked tired, weary even. The tubes in his nose and arms looked scary, I just remembered what the nurse said, that he looked worse than he actually was.

"I'm going to stay with him," Sandra said.

No one objected. We all knew of her interest in Nate. Besides, we felt someone should stay with him all night. I stayed until the end of visiting hours with Rev. Fisher reading scriptures and praying. On the way home, I had one of my moments again, I guess thoughts of my mom and mamma Williams, and now Nate were too much to bear. Rev. Fisher was understanding of course, but firm with me.

"Derrick, you have to control these feelings of loneliness, God is with you always. Look to him for comfort and security and not people, one day you will have to." Fisher warned.

"I know, it's just something I have never been able to get over. Since I lost my mom, my biggest fear in life is being alone, I can't help it," I said in despair.

"That is of the enemy, God promised he would be with you always. It's right in the Gospel of Matthew, we read it, remember?"

"I know Pastor, I just forget sometime," I resigned.
Reverend Fisher looked at me for a minute and told me that I needed to have more faith, and that comes by reading my bible and attending the classes. He said that I took an incredible leap of faith by surrendering to Christ, but now the work really begins; now I had to stay close to him. After leaving the hospital, we sat in the church parking lot talking for about twenty minutes.

"Derrick, I am going to tell you something that very few Christians have the power to do. Learn to let go of all that you fear to lose in life. Fear of loss is the path to Satan. It is a tool he uses to control us, fear can make you do unspeakable things that you would not ordinarily do."

He was right, all my life I was afraid of losing people. It was the fear of abandonment and loss that made me commit those terrible crimes when we had the family. I knew it was wrong, but I was afraid Nate wouldn't accept me anymore and that I would be an outsider. My mother's death had an effect on me that I had not yet confronted, she was a hopeless drug addict but I knew she loved me and she'd do anything for me. Rev. Fisher was right, that loss had molded me to be emotionally needy; I needed to belong to someone, somewhere anything just so long as I was not alone.

It was hot and muggy when I woke up the next morning, the church's central air was broken and the forecast was projected to be a scorcher. I got up and took a shower and hurried down to the kitchen area to see what mother Vincent may have stirred up, and found no one. I went to the sanctuary to find it also empty; the scaffold was still in place. The next place to check would be Rev. Fisher's office. On my way up, I heard Deacon Jackson on the phone seemingly very upset. He talked to someone about never coming around the church again, and that he would call the police if they did. I immediately thought it might be the strange man in the car Nate and I were trying to avoid, so I listened more. After the phone conversation I walked in pretending that I was just now coming into the room.

"Good morning, Deacon, where is everyone?"

"Oh, they all went down to the hospital."

"Well why didn't they wake me?"

"I had to stay around here, so they figured they would let you sleep, and I told them I would bring you in later."

"Are you ok, sir?"

"Fine! Do you want to go now, because I have a run to make?"

"Well if it is on the way, I could just tag along, no sense in-

"No, you stay here I will be back in about twenty minutes. Mother Vincent left your breakfast on the stove, why don't you eat until I return."

What was I gonna say? The man insisted, so I stayed. As he was leaving, I walked him to the front door of the church to see that same car again parked outside. I tried to stay out of sight as I talked to Jackson as he walked out. I was starting to get angry now. I didn't like the fact of being spied on, I wanted to just walk over and confront the driver.

Once again, it was a clean shaven white male with dark sunglasses speaking into a recording device and taking notes. I peeked through the window and watched as Deacon Jackson walked down the steps and into his car and drove off. Then the unthinkable....the guy got out of his car and started walking toward the church!

****

"Hey Nate, can I speak to you for a minute?"

"Yeah, c'mon in, G, what's on your mind?"

"I was talking to Mike and he kinda filled me in on what's going on with the whole Al thing. Not that I'm not trying to second guess you Nate, but don't you think you're being heavy handed on this one?"

"Hell no! This motherfucker cuffed three hundred grand from me and I ain't taking that, G, I know how you are and you know how I am. I just can't roll with that."

"Yeah, but killing his cousin, Nate, and her thirteen year old kid? What did that accomplish?"

"It lets people know I ain't fucking around, G, I want my damn money and I don't care how many of his family members I have to kill to get it."

I poured myself a glass of Cognac, and tried to reason with him.

"Nate, in life we all make choices. You're probably buying the farm with this one. Now you made this guy sell coke longer than he wanted to, you turn around and bribe his wife into sleeping with you, and you fault him and his family for running off?"

"G, your point is taken, but he stole from me."

"There are only thieves in this room! Wake up, Nate, do you know what we do for a living? We murder, steal, and destroy how the hell can either of us judge this man?"

"Whatever, I'm gonna find his ass and I'm gonna deal with him. You know me, this asshole sealed his fate the minute him and that bitch decided to take my cash."

"What about his family, they don't have anything to do with this."

"Guilty, by association," he said smiling.

"Have you ever thought about the consequences of all of this death and destruction, Nate?"

"Fuck do you mean?"

"Never mind, you've never listened before, why the hell would you listen now? Let this one go Nate, I know it's a chunk of change, but that's exactly what it is to us….change. The family has over seven million dollars stuffed into the count room. Are you really gonna annihilate this man's entire family for three hundred thousand?"

"I would annihilate his entire family for fifty thousand! The shit ain't about the money, G, it's about principle."

I finished the last swallow of my Cognac, sat the glass down on his desk, and walked out. Talking to Nate sometime was like talking to a brick wall, he just didn't get it. He had lost all respect for human life; Nate was more concerned with reputation and making people fear him. There was no reason behind murder now, it was wanton and senseless, at least as I saw it. Just when I thought Nate couldn't go any lower he always seemed to surprise me.

CHAPTER 7

I began to sweat as he walked toward the church. What would I say? How would I handle myself? I figured he would talk to Jackson, but he watched him walk down the street and never approached him. As he began to knock, I wiped the sweat from my brow and peaked at him through a side window. He knocked and knocked, after a few minutes he lifted his sunglasses and looked up toward the roof of the church, and gave a quick panoramic view and started back down the front stairs.

I released the curtain and watched him through one of its folds. As he got into the vehicle, I saw him make a phone call and drive off. Walking back toward the kitchen, all sorts of things went through my mind. Were the powers that be waiting for the right time to arrest Nate and I? Why were they playing this cat and mouse game? Who exactly were they? Only Nate could answer these questions and now he was sick. I never thought one could feel anger and fear all at at once, but I did. The future was so uncertain for Nate and I, and we were constantly on edge about it.

Later when Jackson and I arrived at the hospital, Nate had come around and was trying to talk to everyone.

The nurse had propped his head up and given him some ice chips to eat. He seemed different, more reflective, totally unlike himself.

"Hey man, where have you been?" he said forcing a smile

"At the church, how are you, dude? You are supposed to step down off of those scaffolds!" I said trying to lighten him up.

"Funny! Man, I slipped off that thing and the next thing I remember I'm in here."

Everyone smiled and gave him all sorts of cards, flowers, scripture tracts and the like. Sandra had been there all night and she looked exhausted. Rev Fisher suggested that we all go get some rest; since Jackson and I had just arrived, I wanted to stay longer.

The doctor had just come in before I arrived and informed everyone that Nate had only suffered a concussion, and he would have to take it easy for a while. Nate had slept for the last day or so, needless to say he wanted company. Rev. Fisher talked everyone into leaving so he could talk to Nate and me alone.

Once everyone walked out, Sandra gave Nate a kiss on the cheek and instructed him to eat the vegetables when dinner was brought in later, and left. Rev. Fisher pulled up a chair next to Nate's bed, I sat down next to him and he gave it to us.

"Boys, there are a few things I want to talk to you about," he said after he exhaled.

"First, that Mullenrand boy, has been transferred to a maximum security penitentiary in Virginia, he has refused to give much information to the authorities about you two. The powers that be believe you two to be dead. Now I am willing to keep your identities secret, but Nathan you are going to have to take this program more seriously. There are powerful people asking questions, but I believe that God will protect you two. I believe he has a plan for you."

"What questions? What powerful people?" I asked.

Rev. Fisher looked down into his lap at his folded hands; I could tell he was burdened with this whole situation.

"The F.B.I, son, they haven't come to me directly, but they have approached a few of the congregants, and some of my minister friends. They have been asking questions all over the community, and especially in Chicago."

"What exactly are they asking?" Nate asked.

"Well, they are trying to find out if any of the people that were involved with your   previous gang are still alive."

"Well, we were not a gang Rev. we-

"Rev. Fisher, what are your people saying to them?"

"Son, my friends don't know anything, and if they did they would not tell them. We are all trying to help you boys, and ministers must hold these things in the strictest of confidentiality. Now once you boys walk away, you are on your own."

Nate and I just looked at each other; we both were thinking the same thing. We both figured eventually we would be discovered, however we also knew that Rev. Fisher and the program was the best thing going for us.

"What else did you have to tell us, sir?" I asked.

"Well, I recently got my test results back and my cancer has resurfaced. I will have to have more treatments, which means I will have to take a sabbatical, I am leaving the program and you two in the hands of Deacon Jackson for a while."

****

"Mike got a tip on a guy who might have some information on Al's whereabouts Nate," Dana said dutifully.

"Who is it?"

"A pastor, a guy Al's wife confided in a lot. Her mom was a member at their church, and word has it their family talked to him about everything, he just may know something."

"Cool, then we will have to pay the good Rev a visit, huh?"

"Well maybe so, but do we really want to get rough with a minister?" Dana asked.

"Now there you go! I don't give a shit who it is, I want info on my money, and if he got it, he's gonna give it up or else!"

"C'mon Nate, this guy is a preacher. I think we should question him, but let's shy away from the rough stuff," Mike said walking into the office.

"Shy away from the rough stuff," Nate said folding his arms in feigned thought.

"Shy away, I'm sure you are right Mike. I really think maybe we should take it easy huh? Maybe go there have a little bible study, talk a little religion and somewhere in there, maybe just mention the fact that a motherfucker took off with almost three hundred thousand dollars of my money. But we won't offend him just ask carefully, I'm sure you are right about that, Mike. Wait, I have a better idea, and I'm just brainstorming here, while we are there, why don't we just make a donation to the church you know show how nice we really are!" Nate said condescendingly.

"No, wait, let's do this. When we go there, why don't we have all of our guys surrender and just shut this whole organization down, forget the money and join church! Pete get me G on the phone, find out where he is and tell him we are all gonna quit this shit and join church! How is that Mike, is that nicey nicey enough? Is that soft enough for you?"

"Nate, I didn't mean-

"Hey fuck you! If I'm not mistaken this is a criminal organization, and I am the head of it! I don't believe you people, I lost three hundred grand, and you all want me to kiss everyone's ass while I try and find it? You fuckers better go kick some rocks, I want my motherfucking money, and if this asshole doesn't sing the way I want him to, I will cut his fucking throat right in that damn church, do you understand?" Nate screamed.

Everyone looked down at their feet somberly.

"Do you understand?!" Nate hollered.

"Yeah, we got it." Dana and Mike said in unison.

"Good, now get me a couple of guys, and get dressed, we going to church," Nate said smiling.

****

The same night Nate was discharged from the hospital, he told me he wanted to talk about some things. I could tell he had changed, his mood, his thoughts, had all changed. Nate actually seemed happy to get back to the church. Sandra had prepared dinner for us, and cleaned up our area upstairs. My mind was going a million miles a minute, thinking about our futures. I was worried about Rev. Fisher and his health, Nate and his mental well being, and if we would ever be able to live normal lives. Nate took his medication and went into the kitchen to talk to Sandra. I sat down in our room and began to think about the whole F.B.I thing. Somehow, I felt Nate and I were just spinning our wheels, I figured when it was all said and done we would still end up in a jail cell.

Hey G, you ok?" Nate said peeking around the door.
"Yeah, what's up?"
"Nothing, just wanted to talk, that's all," he said throwing his suitcase on the bed, and kicking off his shoes.
He walked over to the nightstand and picked up my bible and surveyed it.
"How often do you read it, G?"
"Sometime, when I'm feeling down, it helps me make sense of things when things don't make sense."
"Humph, aint that the truth."
"Nate, what's bothering you?"
Nate walked over and sat on the edge of the bed, placed his elbows on both legs, folding his fingers together and looked down at the floor.
"G, I'm at my wits end. I am so tired mentally I am dizzy. Do you know I didn't get a minutes rest while I was at that hospital?"

"Nate you slept for over a day, you had a concussion."

"G, I slept, but I didn't rest."

"It's Gabby and the baby, isn't it?"

"No, I am at peace with that now. I'm just tired man, tired of running, tired of hiding, tired of lying. I'm thirty-two years old and I don't have anything to show for my life, all I have is the clothes on my back. If I had died in that hospital, the state would've had to bury me, and with my past, they probably would have thrown me down a manhole."

"Don't talk like that Nate-

"It's the truth, G, when I look back over my life I can't think of one thing that I am proud of, besides my high school diploma. I fucked my life up, man, royally! All that money and shit we had is gone. I have no skills, no training in shit. I'm a fucking loser living in a church attic! I like this girl Sandra, G, but what the hell can I give her? Now I got the fucking F.B.I looking for me!"

"We don't see you as a loser, Nate," I said trying to console him.

"It's not about how you see me, G, it's how I feel about me! I don't feel good about myself, man. I can't even get a job mopping a floor, who the hell is gonna hire me to do anything? I gotta spend my life duck, dodging and hiding from the law and my past, and to tell the truth, I don't think I can do it!" Nate said as tears welled in his eyes.

I felt bad for him, and I wanted to dispel some of the things he said, but he was right. I remember momma Williams once taught us that if you can't say anything good, it's best not to say anything at all. So I walked over and sat next to him on the bed, and threw my arm around his shoulder.

"Hey Nate take it easy, it's been a long week. Let's get some sleep, dude, maybe you will feel better after service tomorrow."

"G, there is no tomorrow for me anymore. I am living on borrowed time."

The next morning I was awakened by the smell of breakfast as usual, mother Vincent was making waffles, homemade style! As I got a shower and prepared for breakfast I noticed Nate had already made his bed and gone.

"Good morning mother Vincent, where is Nate?"

"Oh mornin' honey, he and Deacon Jackson are in the sanctuary, preparing for service. You eating this morning?"

"Yeah, I will be right back I wanna see what they are doing."

When I got into the sanctuary, Deacon Jackson and Nate where laughing, talking and getting along great.

"Good morning Derrick how are things?" Rev. Fisher said walking up behind me.

"Oh, they are fine, Reverend. Just noticing how Nate and Deacon are getting along."

"Yes, that young man is really coming along. I am very proud of him. I was at the Junior College this morning and I saw some pamphlets on some of their Allied Health programs, and I thought of you. Maybe you might want to look into them." He said as he handed me the papers.

"Nursing, Radiology Technology, Respiratory, thanks Reverend, I will look at them, but it has been a long time since I've been in school."

"I know, but is anything too hard for God?"

"No, I guess not. What about Nate, you think he would be interested?"

"Well, I think Nate's destiny lies along a different path," he said looking at Nate and Jackson in the sanctuary.

"When do you begin your treatments?"

"Tomorrow morning, I haven't written to Jeremiah to tell him yet. I don't want to worry him."

"Pastor, we are all prayerful, for your health."

"It's gonna be tough Derrick, I am not too fond of those treatments, I am not sure if I can handle the physical and emotional stress of it all again."

"Is anything too hard for God?" I said with a smile.

"No, I guess not," he said smiling.

Reverend Fisher was really worried about his health, concerned about what would happen to the church, what would happen to Nate and I, his son, the congregation and all. He had been so wonderful to me and Nate that I felt his burden.

Service started as usual; the Deacon opened with prayer and scripture, the choir marched in as usual, we had announcements, testimonials same as always. But this time the difference was Nate, he seemed so in tune with the service, yet very solemn.

I noticed when the choir sung, he clapped his hands and stood to push them on, when we had altar prayer he actually came up for prayer along with the others! Usually before Reverend Fisher gives his sermon, Sister Vincent sings a nice song; but this time Sandra was tapped to sing the meditation song. I've never been to any of the choir meetings, so I have no idea how they decide what is sung. But this time Sandra sang the same song that was sung at momma Williams' funeral "There's not a friend like the lowly Jesus." I looked back at Nate to give him an eye shot to see if he remembered the song and saw him hunched over balling like a baby. I stood up to go to him and Deacon Jackson motioned for me to sit down. He walked over to me and whispered that the spirit was working with him.

"If you go over there, you will interrupt God's business, leave him alone."

It seemed the whole church was transfixed to Nate, you see Nate had been so hard hearted that some thought he had no chance at redemption, so this was something to see.

I was worried about him and I wanted to help him out. I looked up at Rev. Fisher and he stood up from his seat with his eyes wide open, he even looked surprised. Sandra had her eyes closed singing as tears streamed down her face. Rev. Fisher had said later that night that God was using her to soften Nate's heart. As Sandra neared the end of the song, Deacon Jackson stood up and walked over to Nate and gently held out his hand.

"It's time son."

Nate looked up, his face soaked with tears, and gently nodded his head. He stood up and took hold of Jackson's hand and walked up to the front of the church. The entire congregation erupted in raw emotion, Rev. Fisher shot up and held his hands up and praised God in unison with the rest of the church. It was one of the most emotional moments I had ever witnessed. Sandra finished her song, and looked at Nate and was so overcome with emotion, that she danced and shouted praise to God.

Rev. Fisher came down and gave Nate a hug that seemed to last almost a minute. One of the other Deacons handed Rev. Fisher the microphone and Fisher spoke to the congregation.

"You see, this is what I have been teaching. God specializes in impossible things. Son, I love you and I love what God has done with you," he said in between sobs and sniffs.

It is customary at our church for the newcomer to Christ to say the sinners prayer with the pastor, but this time Nate got on his knees at the altar and talked to God in his own way. I was sitting in the front row near the deacons so I could hear his prayer.

"God, I am so sorry! I have been a dope dealer, a killer and I have had men killed. I have done unspeakable things in your sight, but I believe you can redeem me; I stretch my hand and heart out to you and ask you to come into my heart. I am tired, I can't live the way I have lived, I admit I hated you for taking my momma, and my wife and child, but I realize that the failure was never in you, it was I. Come into my heart Jesus and change me, change my life and I will do all that I can to sin no more!"

I had never seen my brother so humbled before, he was never going to be the same again, and I thank God I was there to witness it, the date was September 24th 1999.

****

As Nate and his henchmen drove toward the church, Nate took a 9 mm pistol from Dana, slid in a clip and cocked the pistol and placed it in the small of his back.

"Y'all can leave your shit in the car, we ain't trying to go up in here like the National Guard, I'm the only one that needs to pack," Nate said adjusting his tie.
It was after service and Nate had called ahead to schedule a meeting and told the pastor it was concerning his "spiritual stability."

Being a pastor, the man scheduled the meeting.
A young woman escorted Nate and his "entourage" to the pastor's office.

"Well, hello young man, are you the one who called?"
"Yes sir, this is a nice church you got here," Nate said conning the older man.
"Well thank you, my name is Pastor Sinclair….and you are?"
"Lester, and these are my friends," Nate said extending his hand for a shake.

The man shook Nate's hand and could feel something was wrong, yet invited him into his office anyway.
"How can I help you, son?" the older man asked curiously.
Nate took a seat as his brood of criminals circled around him looking around the man's office, obviously in unfamiliar surroundings.

Nate just looked at the old man, and gave a sly smile. The old man's posture changed from one of a caring soul to one of nervous apprehension. Suddenly, the old man knew. He knew Nate was not there for anything spiritual, he knew he was in the presence of evil and called Nate on it.

"What exactly are you here for? Cause I have another appointment soon and I can reschedule if you-

"Let's cut the bullshit, old man, I don't want to be here any longer than I have to. One of your members sold drugs for me and skipped off with a large sum of my cash. Do you know who I'm talking about?"

"Yes, Albert and his wife, what do you want from me?"

"All I want from you preacher is the truth. I want to know where they are; now I am prepared to offer you and your congregation one-thousand dollars for this information," Nate said grabbing a stack of cash from Dana and placing it on the pastor's desk.

"No thank you," the old man said pushing the money back towards Nate

"Make it twenty-thousand," Nate said smugly.

"You don't have enough money to make me tell you something like that."

"Non-sense!" Nate said full of pride.

The old man leaned back in his leather chair folded his hands in his lap, now comfortable with the situation and spoke.

"Son, I don't know where they are. And if I did, I wouldn't tell you for a million dollars. There is no way I would sell someone out to killers for money, now you get your gang bangers out of my office and God's house before I call the police," the old man said with confidence.

Nate reached in the small of his back and grabbed his gun and aimed it at the old man and cocked it.

"You talk that shit to me, old man, without a gun in your hand?" Nate said now angry.

The old pastor looked at Nate and the gun and smiled.

"Son, you don't scare me, I have served this country in Korea, and Vietnam. I have killed more men than you can imagine. Since then, I have made my penance with God, he's my friend, and I trust him and I know he loves me. Now you can pull the trigger I'm to the point I am not afraid of death, but I caution you; if you murder the man of God in God's house, he will put a burden on you that your little shoulder's could never bear. Now I don't have any information to give you, but you do have a decision to make, either get up and get out of my office and off these premises or….pull the trigger."

Nate drew the gun back from the preachers face and put it back in his pants.

"I'll keep my eye on you, old man, and if I find out you lied to me about knowing anything, I'm gonna come back and next time I won't be so nice," Nate said a bit embarrassed.

The old man clearly showed him up in front of his henchmen; Nate was a bit afraid of what the old man told him but wouldn't let on that he was.

The old man nodded and smiled, allowing Nate to save his face.

"I will pray for you, son," the old man said as Nate and his people walked out of the office. Now Nate was really angry and someone had to pay.

Chapter 8

Over the next year or so, Nate had thoroughly entrenched himself in the bible, and the teachings of Rev. Fisher. Nate would go along with him for his treatments, and he would teach Nate life lessons and church history. The F.B.I guy would still come around from time to time, but we didn't care. Things were going right and Nate always said our fate was in God's hands now. Nate and Sandra started dating heavily, and I started school at Joliet Junior college, for nursing.

Things were going pretty well, Nate had changed so much I didn't know him; he stopped calling me G, and started calling me by my name. He prayed every night, and before each meal. He fasted regularly, and even prayed a few times at the morning services. In fact, the only thing that was a holdover from the old Nate was his workout regiment, and his fondness for his beloved White Sox.

He used to always say that we were entering a new millennium, and we all should renew ourselves to Christ. He grew in Christ faster than I did; in fact everything in his life seemed to be on a fast track. He seemed impatient, and always talked about how tomorrow is not promised, and that we should make good on today, cause that's all we had as children of God. He always asked Rev. Fisher when God would reveal his ministry to him. Rev. Fisher always taught that everyone God brings to himself he gives a ministry. And it took several months before it happened for Nate, then on June 18th 2000, Nate's ministry walked into the church.

"Hey Nate, I think someone is at the church door, you wanna grab it?" Deacon Jackson asked.

"Sure."

Nate walked toward the door and opened it; on the other side was a ghastly sight. There stood a young man seemingly in his thirties that looked like a bum. He reeked of alcohol and he was white around his mouth clearly from smoking crack. His posture was slumped and looked as if he had not bathed or slept in weeks.

"Uh, hi is Sandy around?"

"No, she's at work. May I ask who you are?"

"It's her brother, Ernest, just tell her Ernie was by."

But before Nate could say another word Deacon Jackson maneuvered himself in-between Nate and the door to address the man.

"Boy, I thought I told you never to darken this door again?" he said angrily.

"But dad, I aint lookin for no handout. I'm hungry. I just wanted a few dollars to get something to eat."

"Liar! Don't talk that drug talk to me, you looking for dope is what you want! And ain't nobody got none for you here, now get!"

"But dad I-

"Nathan, call the police!"

"But Deacon, maybe we got something for him to eat, let me just look in the fridge-

"Get the hell outta here boy!"

The young man turned quietly, and started away sheepishly. Deacon Jackson grabbed the door from Nate and slammed it shut and turned the lock afterward.

"Hey, Deacon go easy on him. We got plenty of food back there, we could have given him a plate," Nate tried to reason.

"Nathan, that boy is a hopeless junkie, he been on dope for almost twenty years! Hell he's probably one of your old clients!"

That cut Nate, He took a deep breath and gathered himself again.

"God can help him, Deacon, give him and God a chance."

Jackson looked at Nate with a scowl and walked away.

Needless to say, as soon as I got home from school, Nate told me all about it.

"Derrick, I think he's crackin, he had that look you know," Nate said sorrowfully.

"Stay out of it, Nate, that's family stuff. Jackson and Sandra obviously know about it, let them handle it as a family," I tried to reason.

"Yeah I know but, Jackson talked like the boy was beyond help."

"Nate, they are probably ashamed of him, that's why they haven't said much about him."

"But that's their blood, man, how can they hold out all of this hope for you and me, and just throw him under the bus?"

"Stay out of it, Nate."

"I'm just gonna talk to Sandra about it, that's all. I promise."

I pulled out my books, and began to read as Nate walked out of the door, I knew what he wanted to do, I just wasn't sure if he should or not.

But as with everything, before he went to Sandra he went to Rev. Fisher for advice.

"I mean, he was really barking at him, Pastor, I didn't even know about him."

"I did, that young man has been on drugs for a long time, Nathan. We tried to help him several times, but nothing worked. He always used the church for money and went back to his drugs. It's a sad situation, I have prayed for him for years, we all have."

"Maybe I can help him?" Nate said cautiously.

"Perhaps."

"But then if I fail, Deacon Jackson and Sandra will probably give me the old I told you so."

"Perhaps."

"But this might be what God has for me, you know with my history maybe I might be the one that can help lead him to Christ."

"Perhaps."

"But what if I fail, what if things don't work out? It's probably gonna take a lot of work and time, huh?" Nate asked.

"Perhaps," Rev. Fisher said once again.

"Is that all the advice you have, pastor? Is that all you can say is perhaps?" Nate said discouraged.

Rev. Fisher got up from his desk and walked over to sit next to Nate on the couch in his office. He had lost all of his hair, and quite a bit of weight from his cancer treatments and was weak. He took a deep breath and spoke to him.

"Nathan, I am so proud of you. It seems like only yesterday when I picked you boys up from the hospital and brought you here. I have advised you in many things, but now I must decrease so that Holy Spirit might increase."

"Huh?" Nate said confused.

"It's time for you to go to God for yourself, Nathan; you have to let God instruct you in these things. Go to him in prayer about this matter, and I am positive he will give you the answer." He said fatherly. That night happened to be Nate and Sandra's "Date Night," they both set aside a day a week for them to go out alone and get to know each other privately. Nate picked this night to inquire about Ernest, but he wanted to make sure Sandra was relaxed, calm, and in an even tempered mood, because like Nate, she was known to be a bit outspoken.

He picked a quiet little Italian restaurant in Orland Park, Sandra liked Italian food. They small talked about the church, their pasts, work, and the joys of children (a great topic for most women), and then Nate hit her with it.

"There was a visitor for you today at the church," Nate said with caution.

"Really, who?" Sandra replied sipping her coffee.

"A guy named Ernest, he said he was your brother."

"Oh, yeah he is. What did he say?" she said trying to keep it casual.

"Nothing much, he asked for you, I told him you were still at work. Then your father came to the door."

"We better get the check, Nathan, it's starting to rain," she said now uncomfortable with the conversation.

"I didn't know you had a brother, why didn't you ever tell me?" Nate said smiling trying to keep the mood light.

"Uh, we never got around to it."

"Is he older or younger?"

"Nathan, I'd rather not discuss this right now, ok?" she said agitated.

Nate was tired of playing cat and mouse and got straight to the point, no sense in playing with her emotions, he thought.

"Sandra he didn't look well, and your father really got angry with him. I thought maybe-

"Yeah well we have some family issues, no big deal," she said dismissively.

"I understand, is he on drugs Sandra?"

"Nate, I told you I don't want to talk about this right now."

"Now is as good a time as any, besides we should not hide things from each other, I've told you-

"I'm not hiding anything; I just don't want to talk about it. I can't believe you are going to force me to talk about this," she said now visibly agitated and trying to keep her voice down.

Nate took a deep breath and put his head down.

"I want to try and help him, Sandra," Nate said quietly.

"Yeah well, we all have tried that. He's gotta want help, Nathan."

"Maybe this is what God has, maybe I am the one that can reach him. I know about these issues, believe me."

"Maybe that's the problem, you think you know everything. My father and I will handle it, it's a family issue," she snapped.

Now Nate was hurt, he was only trying to help.

"Oh, yeah I saw what a wonderful job you and Jackson are doing with him," Nate said sarcastically.

"You asshole!" Sandra said through gritted teeth, as she grabbed her purse and shot up from the booth.

"Sandy wait, don't leave," Nate said throwing money on the table trying to catch her.

Sandra hustled past customers in the restaurant, and headed toward the exit. She pushed the double doors open and marched down the street as the rain mixed with fresh tears streamed down her cheeks.

"Sandra, wait! Slow down, wait! I'm sorry, wait for me!" Nate shouted down the street, now jogging to try and catch up.

Onlookers pointed at them and held their umbrellas to see what was about to happen.

Nate finally caught up to her and whirled her around with manly strength.

"I'm sorry. Please don't be angry with me. God has put it on my heart to help him, but I want your support, I love you!" Nate said loudly, as people stood and pointed and whispered.

"I love you too!" she said smiling.

They both kissed passionately, now drenched in the rain. Onlookers started to clap and cheer at the romantic scene, some of the women wiped tears from their faces, as guys smiled and guided their dates toward the restaurant. Nate and Sandra stood there kissing before he hustled her toward the car.

****

Nate walked into the enormous office and placed his gun on the desk, and took a drink of Cognac he had poured earlier. Anger engulfed him as he contemplated whether or not he would kill the young family when he found them. He thought I was right, three-hundred thousand was a mere pittance compared to the millions they warehoused on the compound, but he had been disrespected, outwitted by a square and he simply couldn't have that. He walked over to the thermostat and adjusted the temperature of the office; he always liked it warmer than me, who had adjusted it earlier. Nate missed his mother, and longed for her warm tender motherly advice and guidance. But he was no fool; if his mother were alive she would be vehemently ashamed of his lifestyle, and choices. The situation had him backed into a corner; he now realized that he had to kill him. All of his underlings were aware of the situation, and nothing short of death would be respected, and in his line of work, respect was everything.

"Hey, you in here?" I said knocking and opening the door simultaneously.

"Yeah, come on in," Nate replied dryly.

"Jon says we are nearing forty million in the count room," I said looking around the office.

"Yeah, I know. When you get a chance send Dana in, would you?" Nate replied

"Nate, I heard what happened today at the church."

"Shit, here we go," Nate said looking up at the ceiling and exhaling deeply.

"Hey, man, you don't have to worry I didn't come in here to lecture you."

"Good," Nate said sharply

"I just want to make a statement and get a promise from you."

"What is it, G?"

"I know you Dana and Mike are like a runaway train with this Al thing, and whatever I say won't matter much, it never does. All I want from you, Nate, is a promise that you won't kill this man and his wife and children."

"G, you know I can't and won't promise that. This man stole a ton of money from me, now what crime family would allow that to happen and just forget about it? You are asking me for the impossible, hell if he stole that kind of money from a bank or a government, the F.B.I and A.T.F agents would have his ass, and you know it. They are the law, G, I'm a criminal and you want me to just eat it?" Nate said incredulously.

"Cool, point taken. But consider this; what if momma Williams was alive she would not agree to any of this shit, but would she really want her son to murder a family for money? The love of money is making us all act like savages, Nate, and it's not worth it."

Nate unbuttoned his shirt exposing his muscled chest, and flopped down on the couch.

"Ok G, you got it. I won't hurt him and his wife and children, I promise," Nate said seriously.

"Good, I appreciate that," I said heading toward the door.

"Oh, send in Dana for me ok," Nate said motioning for his dog to come to him.

"Yeah, no problem."

Nate grabbed a cigar and lit it as he cuddled his massive Rottweiler.

"Yeah, what's up Nate?" Dana asked.

"Come in and close the door."

Dana came in and sat down next to Nate on the couch, and gave him her undivided attention.

"I talked to a couple of G's intelligence guys, I want you to take a trip to the west side for me…….."

Chapter 9

Sandra talked to her father about Nate helping Ernest; to say that Deacon Jackson was against the idea was an understatement. But Sandra had a way with her father, as most girls do. She was able to convince him to at least give the idea a try. Sandra had a sit down with Nate and filled him in on Ernest. As it turns out, Ernest had a wife and child living on the west side of Joliet. She had long since thrown him out because of his drinking and drug abuse. Ernest had always drunk heavily, but when his wife lost their second child, it sent him over the edge.

He started hanging out with the wrong crowd, and got turned on to crack. He took a random drug test administered by his long time job at the fastening plant and pissed hot. Needless to say that he lost the job and from then on, everything went downhill. He went from reefer, and an occasional cocaine toot, to crack cocaine. He began physically abusing his wife, and acting strange and aloof. He was incarcerated for three months in the county jail for some petty theft. After serving his sentence, he never went back home.

He lived from pillow to post, and mostly on the streets. His wife took on two jobs to take care of herself and their child, but she never gave up on him. Linda, his wife, joined the church, but can't attend regularly due to work, and babysitter issues. Deacon Jackson and Sandra give her money from time to time to help her with expenses, but the most pitiful aspect of this whole story is Ernest's son, Jacob, who really loves his dad. He spends most of the time talking about him, and asking for him. Ernest's absence has devastated him, and left a deep void in that family. This is one of the most understated problems the effect of drugs has had on this society; how it destroys families.

When Nate heard all of this, it burdened him so much that he cried, he felt directly responsible, having been a drug distributor. He didn't go to Ernest directly at first; he wanted to go to talk to his family. So Nate, Sandra and I paid them a visit.

"Now Nathan, Linda is a very emotional woman, so kinda go easy ok?" Sandra warned as she drove.

"Ok," Nate responded gazing out of the window.

He seemed so preoccupied, deep in his thoughts, and very distant. Nate had been going through emotional ups and downs lately. He would be so optimistic joyous one minute, and down and solemn the next. I figured this was one of them, so I decided to change the subject.

"Hey Nate, the Sox look good this year, huh?" He always liked to talk about the White Sox.

"So far, I'm not surprised, though. I knew we would get better now that we got rid of Manuel, Ozzie can coach circles around him," Nate said sitting up and shifting emotional gears.

"Hey babe, you're a White Sox fan, right?" he asked Sandra.

"Well, I'm not into baseball much. It's kinda boring, now basketball is my sport," she said smiling.

"Really, you a Bulls fan?" I asked.

"Nah, the Lakers baby, I just love Shaq. He's like a big teddy bear," she said, excited.

Nate slumped back down in his seat and looked back out of the window.

I noticed the closer we got to the house the worse the area became. The street the house was on was littered with broken glass, guys hanging around drinking, stray dogs, all the trappings of ghetto life. And Linda, being the only white woman on the block stuck out like a sore thumb. She was in front as we pulled up, attempting to mow the lawn. The little boy, Jacob, was on his knees, playing with some cars and trucks Linda had put out for him. Upon meeting her, I noticed that she looked beaten, tired, and depressed. She tried to muster up a smile and greet us graciously, but I knew it was all an act. She was a victim, and her husband's drug abuse, coupled with the tasks of single parenthood had long taken its toll on her.

"Well hello girl, how have you been?" Sandra said trying to hide her sorrow.

"Ok, just trying to get this grass done," Linda replied trying to push her hair aside and wiping the sweat from her face.

"And look at you, young man you are really growing up! He seems to have grown an inch since last week, Linda," Sandra said, picking up little Jacob.

After introductions, and exchanging pleasantries, Nate took the lawnmower from Linda and finished cutting the grass for her. After small talk in the yard, we all went into the house to address the issue at hand. The house, a bit unkempt had a bit of a smell. We sat on the couch and Linda went right into it.

"Have you seen him, Sandra?" Linda asked

"No, but Nate talked to him the other day. He came over to the church while I was at work. He and Dad had some words and he left. We haven't seen nor heard from him since," Sandra said

Linda wiped a tear away that had welled in her eye and slightly turned away, to hide it from Jacob.

"Hey Jacob, I see you like cars. Do you have any in your room that we can play with?" I said. This was a discussion I didn't feel Jacob should be part of. The boy's demeanor seemed great, he was well cared for and polite, but you could tell that Ernest's absence had left a void.

"I don't know what else to do, Sandra. I'm just tired, tired of lying to Jacob, tired of being the sole provider, tired of hoping and praying that he will come back. I love him dearly, but this has been going on for two years now, and I just want my marriage to work, but he is leaving me no choice...." Linda began to sob as Nate and Sandra just looked at each other unable to find the right words.

Nate got up from the loveseat and sat next to Linda on the sofa with an action figure in his hand, and put his arm around her.

"Linda, God is going to fix this. Don't you dare give up on God, him, or your marriage."

"How can you be sure?"

"I want to help him, I'm going to help him. I have prayed and asked God for guidance, and he has assured me that Ernest will come around. I am going to devote all of my time to helping you all. Starting first thing in the morning, but I need you to get it together, I need you to be strong just a while longer. I have talked to Rev. Fisher and he has promised me that he will share the church's resources to save Ernest, and this family."

"And I will do more also, Linda, my father and I have helped, but we have been feeling sorry for ourselves also. Instead of really getting involved, we have been hiding this issue because we were ashamed of the situation, but all of that will change. I want you to allow Jacob to come stay with me for a week. A few of the sisters from the church will come over every day to help you get things squared away around here, ok?"

"What about your job?" Linda asked.

"I have put in for a leave of absence. Right now, I have to help save my brother and this family. Nathan has made me realize that outside of God, we as believers are all that we have, and we should stick together in Christ."

Linda buried her head in Nate's chest and wept uncontrollably. As Sandra got up from her seat and came over to help console her, I gently pushed the door closed and wiped a tear from my eye while Jacob was not looking. Things were all in place, now comes the hard part.

****

Nate looked out the kitchen bay window at the vicious dogs playing in the yard as he took sips of his coffee. It was a balmy morning and the windows were wet from the night's rain. Gabriella and the rest of the house was still asleep, Nate's anger had grown and he was ripe for revenge on a family that had one upped him as whispers of it had trickled through the crime society.

"Mornin' boss man," Dana said with a smile.

"Mornin my ass, you take care of that thing last night?" Nate barked.

"Yeah, she in the dungeon, we got in late and I didn't want to wake you up," Dana said.

"Good, talk to me, what she know?" Nate said as he sat at the kitchen table to talk to Dana.

"She claim nothing, but when we got there, bitch had new shit all through that place; stove, refrigerator, dinette set and shit. Bitch claim she hit the lotto, but she lying, you can tell," Dana said as she poured cereal into a bowl.

"You find any cash in the crib?"

"Nah, we went through that motherfucker with a fine tooth comb, we didn't find shit."

"Yeah, punk ass bought his momma some new shit with my money," Nate said reflecting.

"What kinda shape she in?" he asked.

"She cool, we slapped her around a bit to get that info, but other than that she all good." Dana said slurping cereal from the spoon.

"Alright good, get word out to all of our people in the area, and in Wisconsin and Indiana, let them all know I got his momma," Nate said stirring his coffee.

"You gonna talk to her, try to get some info?"

"Not really, just scare her up a bit for now."

"Then what?"

"Well she the worm that's gon' bring in the fish. When he find out we got his momma, he gon' come in. Tell everybody he got a week, and if he ain't here with my fucking money we gon' bury his momma.....alive," Nate said casually.

"You really gonna do it if he don't show?" Dana asked curiously.

Nate simply winked his eye at her as he sipped coffee.

****

We were all on the same page, we were all gonna pull together and help Linda and Ernest save their marriage, and attempt to get Ernest off drugs. But that was gonna be easier said than done. We all wanted to do the right thing, but the question was, were we up for the challenge? Nate got started right away; he grabbed some guys from the church and began combing the streets looking for Ernest, which was a challenge for him because while looking for Ernest, he also had to stay out of sight of our friend in the car. He began on Jefferson Street, asking people who were obviously in the "life", if they had seen Ernest. He went to some pretty tough areas, and I was really worried about him. I tried to go with him some of the times, but I would always get the same reply "Between my street knowledge and God's protection, I will be fine." Often, I would tell the guys that went with him to watch out for him and I would just pray. Nate looked for Ernest for a week, then one evening when he and I went together, we hit pay dirt. There was this god awful housing project we went to in this really rough area. Man was I afraid, I will never forget that night.

We got a tip from a guy on Cass street about a place where the "crackheads" hang out to smoke their goodies, but he warned us not to go there unless we were strapped (had guns) because there was one way in, and only one way out! Great, I thought, just what I wanted to hear! I knew Nate was gonna be pumped up to go, but I sure wasn't! At any rate, Sandra gave us her car and I did all I could to talk Nate into letting someone else go in his place.

"Not a chance Derrick, no sense in being afraid. God did not give us a spirit of fear, right?" Nate said smiling.
"I know, Nate, but it's a safety issue, we don't wanna get hurt going down there. It's a rough area, and maybe we should let some of the other guys handle it."
"C'mon Derrick, be cool, dude, God has us. Now we are just gonna go in there, find Ernest talk to him and bring him out, ok?"

I didn't say a word, what would have been the point, his mind was made up. We had dinner at the church, said our prayers for God's protection and got on our way. I surely didn't want to go, but I had to go and watch out for Nate, and keep a lookout for the guy in the car. We drove around for a while looking for the place, we didn't know our way around Joliet like Sandra did, but there was no way Nate was gonna let her go. Finally after about a half hour or so of driving, being lost and getting different directions, we found the place.

Nate and I said a brief prayer before getting out of the car, we told the young man that drove us to be safe and stay alert of his surroundings. We picked up our bibles and headed toward the complex.

****

"Hey Nate, what is this I hear about you having Al's mom in the dungeon, what's up with that?"

"That's right, G, I got her ass down there and if her boy doesn't show up with my cash I'm sticking her ass in a hole," Nate said dryly.

"I thought we had an agreement Nate you said-

"No! I never told you I wouldn't fuck with his mom; I told you I wouldn't do anything to him or his wife and kids!"

"This is insane, I'm gonna go down there and cut her loose."

"No you're not, G!" Nate said pulling his gun out and aiming it at me.

"What the hell is your problem? Oh, you're gonna shoot me now?" I asked incredulously.

He said nothing. He just stood there and thought for a minute.

"No, I'm not gonna shoot you, G," he said releasing the hammer on the gun and drawing it back.

He clapped a couple of times and his two vicious dogs came into the room. And stood guard at the door after he closed it.

"You're gonna stay here and keep Neffi, and Cleo company, until I get back. You make a move to that door, G, and they're gonna tear your ass to pieces," he said taking my gun from me.

"Great, now you're turning on your brother," I said

"Not turning on you, G, I still love ya, you just a little twisted on how shit goes around here, and I think you need a little time to think things over, that's all," he said smiling and walking out of the office from a side door. As Nate traveled down the long corridor that led to the infamous dungeon, he struggled with his emotions. On one hand, he desired to utterly destroy Al and his entire family, on the other, he wanted to let it all go and move on. After all, whatever he did would not bring back his money, and it was tough to murder a man's mother, knowing that he also had one. This was the crime world, and in this world you just don't let a man cuff that kind of cash from you without maximum retaliation. Somebody had to die. If nothing is done, you look soft to your allies and enemies alike; he just couldn't have that.

He walked in the door, and noticed about four or five mafia guys playing cards at one table, Dana flipping through the newspaper, and Mike watching television. The old woman was sitting in a chair with her hands tied behind her and her ankles bound together. Dana had placed a black sack over her head. Everyone jumped to attention and abandoned their previous projects once they saw Nate walk in.

"Alright everybody, get your shit together, it's show time," Nate said grabbing a bottle of Cognac from the table and pouring himself a drink. Everyone scurried themselves together, and gathered around the woman to see what would take place next.

Nate grabbed a joint from Dana and took a long deep drag from it, and threw down a double shot of Cognac. He then held his hand out gesturing for Dana's 9 mm glock. He gathered himself mentally and emotionally and walked toward the woman. There was a dead silence in the room; anticipation filled the air with everyone knowing what must be done, but wanted to see if their leader had the wherewithal to do it. Nate snatched the cloth from the woman's head and began his interrogation.

Chapter 10

As soon as we approached the entrance of the housing complex, two guys that were standing around gathered themselves in front of us blocking our entrance.

"Who the fuck yall here to see?" One of the guys mumbled

"We are here to get our brother," Nate said without looking at him.

"Your brother who?"

"Look they got Bibles man, fuck yall here to preach?" One of the other guys said smiling as the group started to laugh.

"Hey man, I think yall in the wrong place, church down the street."

Nate gave the guy a quick dismissive glance and started toward the entrance again.

"I said, church down the fuckin street!" The young guy said whipping out a gun and drawing it to Nate's face.

Now the old Nate would have made that young boy eat that gun, but this was the new Nate, the God-fearing Nate.

"Cool out, dude, let these squares in man. What's the worse they can do? Gone head man, do your thang, but ain't nobody in there gon' hear you, trust me," another guy said clearly mocking us.

"Shit they could be five-o or something,." another guy yelled from a few feet away.

"Naw, not these dudes, let 'em in, man."

Nate glared at the man that shoved the gun to his face and walked in. I was so relieved, I could have fainted, I thought we were gonna be shot. If I had told those guys who we once were they would not have believed it.

"That was close, huh?" I asked Nate.

He didn't say a word; he immediately started looking around the place. There were children as young as three and four years old playing in the street and it was well after eight o'clock! Guys were shooting dice on the sidewalks, drinking beer from paper bags, women talking and cursing loudly on cell phones as they yelled and cursed at the children. I heard firecrackers going off, and people tossing bottles into the street breaking them, it was horrible. Nate ignored it all as he walked down the street, he was so focused and driven to find Ernest. After walking about three blocks, he started stopping people to ask them where he could find Ernest.

"Can you tell me where to find Ernest?" Nate asked one woman.

"Who the fuck is that, I don't know no damn Ernest," the woman bellowed.

"Thank you anyway," I said

"God bless ma'am," Nate said walking away.

It was starting to get dark now, and the area began to turn for the worse. We heard loud yelling and cursing coming from the end of the block we were walking down, and all of a sudden shots rang out! Nate and I ducked down beside a car, taking cover.

"What the hell?" Nate said trying to look to see what had happened carefully.

"Look Nate, let's just go, we can come back tomorrow in the morning when it's safer. Besides, Ernest might not even be around here," I reasoned.

"We will Derrick, just give me a minute, ok?" Nate said agitated.

People were running and screaming and jerking up children to get to their homes, there was total bedlam. Nate would ask people as they ran by if they knew anything about Ernest. Needless to say no one was listening to him, then one guy did stop just long enough for Nate to get something out of him.

"You mean crackhead Ernie? Shit man he down the block in the sleepshop," The young man said slightly out of breath.

"Sleepshop, what is that?" Nate asked hurriedly.

"You know nigga, the sleepshop! Where all the crackheads get high at," the guy pointed down the street and started running again.

Nate and I scaled down the street with our Bibles tucked under our armpits. We stayed close to the parked cars in case we had to duck again. We saw what looked like a vacant apartment near the end of the block with people coming in and out of it like a subway.

"That's gotta be it," Nate declared.

The closer we got to it, the worse the place smelled. It was one of the most horrific smells that I have experienced; a cross between burnt carpet and rotten flesh! People were laid out all over the place, some were smoking crack from the small pipes; some were eating from trash buckets, while some were just standing up zoned out. Nate and I coughed from the thick smoke in the air, there were people there from all walks of life; guys with business suits on who looked as if they had been there for hours on end, women smoking their rocks while their children played right next to them. I even witnessed women as well as men giving oral sex out in the open, the whole scene was sick!

"There, there he is!" Nate yelled out.

We both hurried over to a man that was laid out obviously high out of his mind, Nate pulled out a small flashlight from his pocket to get a better look, and sure enough it was Ernest!

"Is he ok?" I asked.

Nate took his thumb and index finger and pulled open his eyelids, then felt his neck for a pulse.

"Yeah, just high. Help me get him up," Nate said handing me his Bible.

Nate lifted Ernie up and tossed him dead-man style over his shoulder as I guided him back out of that place.

As we got to the door, we saw Sandra and Rev. Fisher standing outside clearly looking for us.

"Oh my God, there they are," Sandra yelled.

"I thought I told you all to stay at the church," Nate said.

"We were worried; you two have been gone for hours," Rev. Fisher said anxiously.

Nate and I got into the backseat of the car and kind of propped Ernest up between us; and we were on our way out.

"What happened to the brother who drove us here?" I asked Rev Fisher.

"He left, and came back to the church. He said he heard shots, he didn't see you two, so he came back to get us," Sandra said.

"Well, good thing we didn't need him."

"Is he ok?" Sandra asked.

"Yeah, I believe so. I think he is really high, though," Nate lamented.

"God let him be alright," Rev. Fisher said.

Sandra leaned back toward us from the front seat, and gave Ernest a quick look and examined his pulse and breathing.

"Yeah, he's fine. My father and I have seen him in worse shape than this," she sighed.

Nate and I looked at each other in disbelief; we couldn't believe that a human being could be in worse shape than he was without being dead.

Later at the church, we managed to get Ernest conscious. Rev. Fisher talked of taking him to a hospital and getting him checked out. Sandra wanted to check him into rehab immediately, but Nate wanted him to stay with us. He felt that the same program Rev. Fisher used to help us would help Ernest; I was pretty much on the fence. I really didn't know Ernest, therefore, I couldn't really say what would help him or not. After much debate, the crew decided to keep him at the church, Sandra gave him a thorough look-over as far as his health was concerned, and we made a room for him across from Nate and ours. Nate was so excited about helping Ernest; it was a way for him to sort of give back to God and Rev. Fisher for helping him.

"You know, Derrick, I think Ernest is gonna be alright," Nate said proudly.

"Sure, but take it slow, Nate, this guy has been on drugs a long time. So it will probably take a while before he is completely recovered," I cautioned.

"What do you mean?"

"Well, his body has been dependant on chemicals for such a long period of time, and to be honest, we here at the church don't really know too much about chemical dependency and rehab."

"Is there anything too hard for God?" Nate asked.

"No, Nate it's not about that."

"God helped me overcome a lot of things, he can help Ernest also."

"Nate that's because you wanted help, has anyone really asked Ernest if he wants to recover, or have we all just decided to invade his life and make him recover?"

"Now you are being negative." Nate said flatly.

"No, I am not. The first thing the addict must admit is that he/she has a problem. Until then, you're just spinning your wheels with them, I read it in a textbook and-"

"Rev. Fisher always taught us to lean not unto our own understanding, Derrick, you know that."

"Nate, I am not disagreeing with you, just trying to get you to look at this from a different perspective."

Nate got disgusted and walked out of the room. That was one thing that didn't change about him, his stubbornness.

****

The older woman jumped as Nate snatched the piece of duct tape form her mouth. There was old blood that had dribbled from her nose, she was tired and looked every bit her age. She was terrified as everybody gathered around her to get information on her son's whereabouts. The dungeon was cold and dark, and smelled from past interrogations. The windows were wet from condensation. Fear and concern painted the old lady's face as a tear rolled down her cheek.

"Do you know who I am?" Nate asked smiling.

"No," the woman replied.

"Good, we are looking for your son, Al. He disappeared with a large amount of cash of mine, and by you being momma, I figured you would know of his whereabouts," Nate said calmly.

"No, I don't know. I spoke to him yesterday over the phone, but he didn't tell me where he was," the woman said shivering.

"She doesn't know shit, Dana. Momma don't know where he is," Nate said patronizingly.

"Why don't I believe that?"

"I swear, I aint seen him. He left a week or so ago, and-

"You talked to him yesterday, what time was it?"

"Oh, about seven o'clock," the woman said nervously.

"Did you look at your caller Id to see where he was calling from?"

"It's broke, it didn't work. Look whatever he owes you, I can pay-

The whole room burst into laughter, Nate included.

"That's funny lady, you gonna pay back his debt, huh? What are you on lady, disability, social security or some shit? You can't begin to pay back his debt. But I'll tell you what I do know; I know he bought you new shit with my money. And I know you know what he's into, don't you?"

The woman looked around the room trying to stay brave and not appear afraid.

"Yeah you do, so you haven't seen him, huh?" Nate asked once again.

"No, I told you that."

"But you definitely talked to him at eight o'clock, right?"

"Yes, it was eight o'clock cause-

"Now you see there, you just lied. You fucked up, a minute ago you said it was seven o'clock, you lyin old lady," Nate said smiling.

"I was confused, I-

"Shut up!" Nate shouted.

"You want me to show her what we do to liars, Nate?" Dana asked smiling.

"No, we ain't gonna handle it like that at all. I want you to send some guys out and get her something to eat, and a cup of coffee. We gon' take real good care of big mamma, but it's gon' get real bloody in here lady, cause I'm gonna bring each and every family member you have in here and bust them in their kneecaps and torture them until you tell me something, you're gonna talk too. And the longer it takes, the more frustrated I'm gonna get. And when I do find your son, I'm gonna cut his fuckin throat and I'm gonna make sure you watch, and hear him gurgle for life. Don't fuck with me, lady; you won't meet a more evil man, than me until you get to hell," Nate said smugly.

****

After getting Ernest up and around again, we all talked to him about getting his life together and trying to salvage his marriage. He seemed receptive and willing to change, as most addicts do, but the true test is time.

"Sandy, let me ask you a question, just what got Ernest on drugs in the first place, and when did he start smoking?" Nate asked.

"Ernie has always had substance issues, when he was in high school he would do a little reefer from time to time. He hung around the wrong people, guys who were into drugs and hangin out. Then about ten years ago, he started hanging with this guy named Tommy, and they would go to Chicago, and get reefer and they both got turned on to crack out there. And with the usual problems of life, things just spiraled out of control. My father immediately cut him off, but I would always hold out hope for him. We were best friends when we were kids, but drifted apart as he got deeper into drugs. I've been praying for him, Nathan, I hope God will use you to help him."

"Has he ever been to rehab?" Nate asked.

"Never, he never got that far, the longest Ernie has ever been off drugs was a week. Nathan, do you think Ernie ever got high on drugs back in those days that came from you, just asking," Sandra asked cautiously.

"Who knows, knowing how we were rolling in those days, he very well might have been. But that is the past, God has given me a new start in life, and I am confident he will do the same for Ernie," Nate said.

Later that evening after we went to get Rev. Fisher from the hospital from one of his treatments, Nate opened up to me about his fears and told me something I didn't know. He explained how he had not had a good night's sleep in about six months. He told me about horrible dreams he would have on a regular basis. He told me about nightmares of momma Williams, guys he had murdered, and dreams of people chasing him. He said the dreams were so intense that he would sit up most nights reading, afraid to go to sleep.

"Derrick, I tell you these nightmares are horrible."

"Have you talked to Rev. Fisher about them?" I asked.

"Nah, he got enough on his mind, I don't want to burden him with anymore."

"It will pass, Nate. Ask God to help you with them and pray more, they will pass."

"Think I haven't done that? I have prayed and prayed about it, just can't shake them. Maybe it's my punishment," Nate lamented.

"Don't be crazy man, hey how are things with Sandra?" I asked trying to change the subject.

"Things are great; I really care about her, Derrick. I want to ask her to marry me, but I don't have anything to offer a woman."

"Yeah you do, you're a good guy, man."

"Yeah, but I don't even have a job."

"Hey I've been meaning to tell you, there's a job as a cook at the college I meant to tell you about it. Get up with me Monday, and go fill out the application, you might get it."

"Derrick, I don't know nothing about cooking," Nate said smiling.

"You didn't know anything about drugs either; you managed to handle that pretty well," I joked. We both agreed to that, it was great that we could laugh about our past lives, but the joy wouldn't last very long.

Chapter 11

"Hey Nate, I got the kid, what do you want me to do with him?" Dana asked proudly.

"Boy or Girl?"

"Boy, he don't know what's going on. I told him his grandma wanted us to get him."

"Good, is the old lady sleep?"

"Yeah, Mike holla she out like a light."

"Yeah, she tired as hell, and she is about seventy. Ok, take the kid downstairs but don't let him see the old lady till I get down there," Nate ordered.

Nate wiped his mouth from the food he was eating, cocked his handgun and stuffed it in his side holster. When he got into the dungeon, the old woman was slumped over in her chair asleep, and the young boy was in an adjacent room playing a video game.

"We all good in here?" Nate asked.

"It's all good, do your thing," Dana replied.

He instructed one of Dana's mafia guys to go in and tie the boy's hands, and throw a cloth over his head and bring him in.

Once the boy was brought in, Nate instructed his mafia goons to take the boy's pants off to his underwear and strap him down into a chair right in front of his grandmother. Once the boy was in place, the grandmother's cloth was taken off, and Nate threw a glass of water into her face to awaken her.

"Wakey, Wakey, eggs and bakey," Nate said smiling.

The woman shook her head almost exhausted from being tortured and from sleep deprivation the night before. She was surprised at seeing a young child strapped into a chair right in front of her. Nate snatched the cloth away from the child's head, as everyone in the room shifted nervously.

"Grandma!" The child yelled at the sight of the old woman.

"Baby! It's ok, don't worry, and don't cry, it's ok," the woman said trying to console the young frantic child.

Nate stood with his arms folded taking in the sight scowling.

"Alright, alright enough of all this shit," Nate said sliding the child's chair away from the grandmother.

"You monster, you evil bastard! I'll kill you if you harm this boy, he ain't got nothing to do with this let him go!" The old woman screamed through tears and anger.

"You ain't in a position to threaten me, lady, but the kid won't get hurt if you cooperate, so it's your call," Nate said calmly.

The young boy looked back and forth as the two talked, with fear transfixed on his face, there was a feeling of horror in the room, as if something terrible was about to happen. The feeling of dread and hurt engulfed the area, even Dana hoped the woman would tell Nate something.

"Ok, I just don't want you hurtin my boy!"

"Great, and I just want my money. Let's work together, and everybody can go home."

"Ok, the last I heard, he was on his way to Minnesota. I don't know how far he is by now."

A mafia member walked over to Nate and whispered in his ear that the boy's mamma was looking for him and she was going to the police.

"I don't give a shit, when I get my money everybody can go home."

"Do I have your word that you won't hurt my son?" The woman asked desperately.

"On my daughter I promise I won't hurt him," Nate said with his hand over his chest smiling slyly.

The woman certainly didn't trust him, but she was in no position to anger him or bargain with him, she operated on hope and blind faith.

"What do you want me to do?" Dana asked.

"Call all of our people; I want a massive manhunt out for his ass! You're in charge; call all of our people on police payroll, and our guys in Wisconsin also. I want his ass brought back here alive, Dana."

"Okay." Dana said walking away.

"Dana, I said alive!" Nate said emphatically.

****

Over the next three or four months, Nate worked tirelessly with Ernest. They would get up at six in the morning, work out, and eat a hearty breakfast, then get into the bible. They would have long discussions about life, the drug game, and God. Inside, Nate felt responsible for Ernest, he felt he would be paying his debt to the society of people he helped get hooked on drugs. He wanted to make good with Ernest, and show himself that there was some good in him, because sometime he doubted himself.

"I want to thank you for all you have done for me, man," Ernest said.

"Don't mention it, man. It's what we all should do. I want you to be better man. You got a good wife and a great son over there, and God expects great things from you," Nate said encouraging him.

"You think so? I don't think God got too much he expects from me," he said dismissively.

"Why do you say that?" Nate asked curiously.

"Shit Nate, I ain't been nothing to my family but a drug addict these last few years, I'm just keeping it real, I ain't done nothing to make God interested in me at all," Ernest resigned.

"God doesn't operate like that Ernest, Rev. Fisher taught me that God uses people just like you and I to make a difference in the world and in people's lives. I am living proof of that"

Ernest, like many of us, didn't believe it, though. He never saw the glass as half full when it came to his life. Ernest never saw what he could be with God's help; he could only see what he was at that time which is why it really didn't take long for him to fall off the wagon. After only a month or so, Ernest went home to his family, and after being there just over a few weeks, the pressures of life came raging in. Ernest couldn't get work, and his wife started "nagging" him about the bills.

There were shut off notices, and little Jacob was having bedwetting issues. It wasn't long before Nate got the call.

"Nathan, can you come over please?" Linda said over the phone frantically.

"Linda…..it's two a.m. what's going on?" Nate said still half asleep.

"It's Ernest, we had a fight and he stormed out, I don't know where he is."

Nate could barely understand her, she was obviously grief stricken and Nate could tell that something this time was wrong.

"Are you and Jacob ok?"

"Well, he hit me and my eye is swollen. Nate please don't get the cops, just call Sandy and we can work this out please," she pleaded.

"Ok, just calm down. Nobody's getting the cops, I'll call Sandy and we will be right over, ok?"

"Ok, I will be fine just please…."

"Linda, everything will be cool, just stay there!" Nate said.

"Dammit!" Nate said hanging up the phone and tossing the covers from his body.

"Hey, what's up?" I asked now awake and concerned.

"Get dressed, it's Ernest. He and Linda had a fight, he left the house and Linda is hysterical. I'm gonna wash up, call Sandra and let her know what's going on and tell her to get over here," Nate ordered.

"But Nate, maybe we should-

"Look Derrick, just call ok?" Nate said dismissively.

I didn't say anything, I just made the call. I could tell Nate was upset also because he believed that Ernest had really changed. He thought all of the hours of talking and reading the bible, and counseling sessions with Rev. Fisher worked. What Nate didn't know is the road to true recovery is a marathon, not a sprint. It's one day at a time for the rest of your life, and sometime the addict falls off the wagon. There is a fundamental difference between recovering from selling drugs and being a drug addict.

After getting dressed and hustling over to the house, we saw things were a bit worse than Linda had told us. The house was a mess; there was furniture turned over, lamps had been broken, and clothes were thrown everywhere. Little Jacob was sitting on the couch with a toy car and dried tears fixed on both cheeks. Linda's left eye was closed shut, and there were bruises on her right arm and neck. Sandra fought back tears at the thought of her brother causing his family this much grief. I must say I was filled with emotion myself at the sight, but Nate was livid.

"What happened Linda?" Sandra asked.

"I don't know, he got up from the bed and said he couldn't sleep around ten o'clock. He asked me for some money for cigarettes and I told him I didn't have it, that's when he started screaming and yelling. Complaining about not having his own money, and I asked him to be quiet before he woke up Jacob, but he kept yelling. He grabbed my purse and started rummaging through it, when I tried to take it from him, he hit me and we started fighting and throwing things. I can't do this anymore. I swear I just can't," she said sobbing.

Nate snatched the keys from Sandra and stormed toward the door.

"Nathan, where are you going?" Sandra asked.

I knew exactly where he was going.

"Stay here with Linda and Jacob, I'm gonna go with him," I said running toward the door to follow him.

"You know, Nate, you don't have a license, if we get pulled over we are in deep trouble," I said trying to reason.

He didn't say a word he just got into the car and slammed the door. I got into the passenger side and sat there, he didn't say a word the whole time we drove. I knew Nate was going to that God-forsaken housing project looking for Ernest. I was worried because it was real late this time, near 4 a.m., and Nate had his temper on. We came to a screeching halt in front of the project that caught the interest of onlookers. Nate snatched the keys out of the ignition and jumped out of the car. I also whipped out of my side and came around the car anticipating his next move. We jogged across the street to the entrance but this time there was no one at the gate. We both went through and walked down the blocks like men on a mission. Nate walked straight to the area where we had found Ernest before, people where pointing and talking at us as before, but this time Nate took no notice. One guy approached us as we neared the crack den, and asked us who we were.

"We're here for Ernie, man, that's all we want and we outta here," Nate said with a serious glare.

The man gave both of us a once over and stepped aside to let us by. Just as the last time, the stench in the place was awful and cracked out zombies lined the place from wall to wall. We noticed Ernie sitting at a three-legged makeshift table, taking a hit of the pipe and conversing with a guy who looked like a corpse.

"Get your ass up, Ernie!" Nate shouted from across the room, as he walked toward him.

I tried to keep in step with Nate in case he did something that would get us killed, but stepping over cracked out zombies made it a challenge.

"My man, Nate, what's up, dude? I was just telling my guy here-

Before he could get the rest of his sentence out Nate cracked him across the jaw knocking him out cold. People scattered out of the way, as Nate picked up Ernie and tossed him over his shoulder dead man style and turned to me to lead the way out. I started walking toward the door now coughing from all of the smoke, trying to find the way back out through the haze. Once we got outside, people looked at us and laughed at the sight of Ernie tossed over Nate's shoulder like a rag doll.

"Damn! Is he dead?" One guy asked. Nate never said a word he just kept walking.

"What are you doing? Where are we going?" I asked once we got into the car. But he never said a word. As Nate drove he had this stern look on his face as he bobbed and weaved out of traffic. I prayed we didn't get stopped by the cops.

"I'm taking him where I should have taken him in the first place," he finally said.

"And where is that?"

"Rehab!" he said quickly.

As we pulled up to the hospital, I turned to look back at Ernie in the backseat and he was still out cold. Nate hopped out of the car and threw Ernie over his shoulder again and started walking to the facility. I ran up in front of him to open the door for him.

"How did you know about this place?"

"I told you a long time ago, Derrick, I always have a plan B. I felt like there was a chance he might not hold up. Rev.

Fisher told me about this place when I first started out with him."

Nate and I stood him up at registration as Ernie started to come around. We gave all of the pertinent information and some orderly guys came to take him up, and Ernie went ballistic.

"What the fuck you doin'? Let me go bitch!" Ernie yelled as people around the institution started to look and point.

"It's ok, baby boy. They gonna take good care of you here, you ain't ready for the outside yet Ernie," Nate said with a half smile.

"Fuck you nigga! Kiss my ass, fake as Christian boy, I'm gonna get your ass for this shit. You can't put me in here against my will, bitch!"

"As a matter of fact, Ernie, I can. I will come back and check on you in a few weeks, it's cool," Nate said as we started to walk toward the door.

When we got into the car, Nate explained to me how he signed him in under Sandy's name, and how disappointed he was in how Ernie had acted.

"Nate, Ernie is an addict, you gotta understand that," I tried to reason.

"Yeah, but he played me...and you know how I don't like that."

"With our history, it's about time somebody played us, don't you think?" I said jokingly.

Nate just rolled his eyes and didn't respond. I knew then that he was very serious about Ernie's sobriety; it was an area I never treaded again.

****

Nate stood examining the rain as it hit the windows of his office and fogged his windows, he walked toward the bar and poured himself a drink and took a seat. Mike walked in and grabbed a beer and sat down at the bar next to him.

"Dana get back to you yet?" Nate asked without looking up at him.

"Nah, not yet, she on it, though. Last I talked to her she was near Madison, she got a lead that they were staying somewhere near there before they head into Minnesota," Mike said.

Nate nodded in agreement and approval.

"Say Nate, let me ask you a question," Mike asked cautiously.

Nate looked up at him in anticipation feeling his liquor and reefer.

"If we find this nigga, what we really gonna do with him?"

"First off, it ain't if, it's when, second I'm probably gonna kill his ass," Nate said plainly.

"Well, I heard you promised G-"

"I don't give a fuck what I promised G, I'm putting one in his dome."

Mike took in a deep breath, and let it go. He dreaded his next question because he knew the type of reaction it might get, but he asked anyway.

"You think that's a good idea?"

"Nigga, what the fuck you talking about is it a good idea?"

"Well, I was just thinking maybe we could just-"

"Man, get the fuck outta here and make sure them dumb motherfuckers are on their shit downstairs. I got this up here, I'm the boss and I know damn well what the fuck I'm doing."

Mike passively got up from his chair and started toward the door of the office, opened the door sheepishly and walked out. Nate swallowed the last of his drink and leaned back in his chair and looked up at the ceiling. He felt alone in his decision as he began to contemplate the situation. His phone rang.

"Yeah."

"Hey boss, we got a motherfucker here that took some cash from Al a week ago and might have an idea of where he is, what you want me to do?" The voice said over the phone.

"Bring his ass here and use the service entrance, he got family with him?"

"No, but we can get them."

"Good, do that. But remember keep the shit quiet, ok?"

"You got it," the voice said.

****

Over the next couple of months, Nate spent most of his time doing one of four things; dating Sandra, checking on Ernie, spending time with Rev. Fisher, or immersed in the Bible. We hardly spent time together; it was like Nate was working against time or something. Ernie was coming along wonderfully with his treatment and in the program; he really seemed to be a changed man now. Nate felt great about that, and spirits were extremely upbeat. Just as I was going to confront him about us not really spending time together, he let everyone know he had an announcement to make.

"What's all of this about, Nate?" Rev Fisher asked.

"Just make sure you all are there."

After he had many of the core congregation members along with the church staff assembled in the sanctuary, he and Sandra came to the front holding hands and addressed us all.

"I wanted to tell everyone that I asked Deacon Jackson for his daughter's hand in marriage and he agreed," Nate said smiling.

Everyone kind of looked at him without emotion or not much of a response, which briefly puzzled him.

"Oh, then I asked Sandra and she said yes also," Nate said grinning, understanding their pause.

Then everyone burst into congratulatory phrases and hugs, everyone was so happy for them. Everyone pretty much expected it, and so did I, but things seemed to be moving so fast. I mean Nate usually never did things that way, so later that night I approached him about it.

"Hey, Nate, I'm happy for you and Sandra, man, congrats," I said later in the bedroom.

"Thanks man, I guess it's time to bury old memories and move on to new ones, huh?" he said half-heartedly.

"Yeah, it's time for us to really take steps to move on," I confessed.

"How is school coming?"

"It is what it is, I really am happy about my life now, man. I finally feel like I have some control over things."

"You know, Derrick, I wanted to make another announcement but I felt it would have been too much to lay on everyone at once."

"What's up, man?"

"I think the Lord has called me to preach his word," he said somberly.

"Wow, Nate, that's awesome. How do you know?"

"I have a heavy burden for young men; God has placed them so heavily on my heart that I find myself witnessing to them wherever I go."

"Well God has called all of us to witness Nate, but being a preacher is really-

"I know, but a man knows what he knows. I really don't want to lay all of this on Sandra so soon, but I guess I have to."

"Have you talked with Rev. Fisher yet?"

"No I have a meeting with him tonight; I was hoping you would be there with me."

"Sure I will. It would be great."

I could tell he was burdened about things, Nate walked around in a fog most of the time. It was like he was out of body or something. Often, I would catch him staring out of the window or jotting and scribbling down things. And his poison dreams occurred at least three times a week. I would worry about him a lot, but I really couldn't put my finger on what his issue was. Later that night, he gave his news to Rev. Fisher.

As the three of us gathered into his office, I could see Rev. Fisher was a bit weak and had lost some weight.

"How are things Rev. Fisher, are you ok?" I asked.

"Just feeling my age, Derrick, and my illness I guess," he said jokingly.

"Can we get you anything?" Nate asked.

"Nothing right now boys, have a seat," he said gesturing to the sofa in his office.

After settling in and some brief small talk, Nate got right into it.

"Pastor, I feel that God has called me to preach his word, specifically to men," Nate said boldly.

Rev. Fisher looked at him curiously and rubbed his hand over his bald head and spoke.

"Do you know what that means?" he asked.

"I think so."

"Well, you can't think, Nathan. Being a minister of the Gospel requires the deepest commitment, a humble heart, and a mind set aside for God. I want you to read the book of Timothy and ask the Holy Spirit to give you the understanding of what God says a minister of the Gospel should be," Fisher said.

"I have already done that, Pastor, I have prayed and asked God for wisdom and guidance on this matter," Nate said earnestly.

Rev. Fisher looked at Nathan long and hard as he rubbed the underside of his chin, almost studying him.

"Okay Nathan I'll tell you what, you work hard on Ernest and I will give you a ministry here at the church to work on and we will see how you do."

"What ministry?"

"This one, I want you to take over the men's program here at the church. I am going through treatments and you two boys are well and on your way, so I pass the leadership on to you."

"I don't know what to say, Pastor, I am humbled and honored that you would trust Derrick and I with-"

"Not Derrick, just you," Fisher said emphatically.

"Well Pastor, Derrick and I always did things together, you know," Nate said.

"From what I just heard you expressed a call to the ministry, not Derrick. Nathan, this is one thing you and God will do together, and for a while, it will be you and him exclusively. Do you understand?"

"I think so. You will help me, won't you?"

"All that I can, but your path will be chosen by God. Your ministry and call may be quite different from mine, so you will have to pay close attention to hear the voice of God on matters at stake, that's how it works. You may ask my advice on a particular matter and I will give it, but God may want you to go a different route, you must do as the bible says and trust in him and him alone," Rev Fisher advised.

"I see," Was all Nate replied.

I said nothing, I felt good about Nate's new job in God, but Rev. Fisher was right, it wasn't my thing. I just wanted to finish school and find a way back into society. I loved God and what he had done in my life, but ministering wasn't for me. Nate decided that he wouldn't jump in full force until he was married, and had gotten a little further with his mentoring of Ernie who was due to come out of rehab in a week. I wanted to talk to him about how we had not spent any time together, but he was so excited about his life that I didn't want to cast a negative shadow on things.

Over the next few weeks, I buried myself into my studies, and spent little time around the church. I went to the Sunday services, and an occasional bible study or two that was about it. Nate got a job at the college as a cook and talked all the time to the young guys about God and getting saved. To many, he seemed to be a religious fanatic, but some took him seriously and came to the church and made tremendous changes in their lives. Guys like Carlos Perez, who was a hopeless gambler and never won anything. Between the years of 1999 to 2001 he lost around fifteen thousand dollars! Nate and Ernie got him into Gamblers anonymous, and introduced him to God and now he's a new man. Ernie worked hard with Nate to help save guys; Ernie got a job at a stamping plant working nights, so he could help Nate with the ministry during the day. His marriage got stronger, and Linda was forever indebted to Nate, and Sandra adored him for it. Even Deacon Jackson developed a newfound respect for Nate. Rev. Fisher's health started to deteriorate rapidly and he decided it was time to move his son in as successor at the church.

Nate's original plan was to wait and save some money before he married Sandra, but Rev. Fisher's health was getting worse so he decided to marry her as soon as possible because he wanted Fisher to marry them. The church knew that Fisher wouldn't last long and it was a sad hush throughout the congregation. Jeremiah was a younger more daring minister who wanted to take the church to the "next level" as a tribute to his father's work. Jeremiah spent more time working on church business than he did with his dying father, which angered Nate. After Fisher married Sandra and Nate, he rarely made public appearances, or preaching engagements deferring most of them to his son, Jeremiah.

There was an annual men's conference coming up at a local church where Fisher occasionally preaches, but he was too sick to give the message at that conference. Much to everyone's surprise he gave that assignment to Nate instead of Jeremiah, which caused quite a stir.

"How have you been, Nathan, how is married life treating you?" Fisher asked.

"Its fine sir, more importantly how are you? Nate asked handing Fisher a glass of water.

"Fair to midland, I guess. I called you in here to let you know something. I'm not gonna be able to give the men's conference message this year, I don't think. And I am sending a message to the conference directors to expect you as my replacement," Fisher said looking at Nate for his reaction.

"Oh Pastor I don't know, that's usually a huge conference. I don't know if I am ready for something like that," Nate said humbly.

"You aren't, that's why I chose you."

"I don't understand, isn't Jeremiah more equipped for a message like that?"

"Sure he is, but God put you in my heart to do it."

"I'm not sure I understand, sir."

"Help me over to the bed and I will explain."

Nate helped fisher over to his bed and tucked him in. As it was getting chilly, he   brought down the bedroom window then pulled a chair closer to the bed and fixed himself to hear Fisher's explanation.   After adjusting himself in the bed, Fisher began to talk.

"My son Jeremiah is a great speaker. I am so proud of what God has done with him and his gifts and abilities. But Jeremiah is not the preacher that you are."

"What do you mean?"

"Nathan, you have an extraordinary gift, when you teach and preach men are moved. Do you understand?"

"I guess," Nate said humbly.

"When Jeremiah gives a message, people clap and understand, he speaks to their minds and he makes a strong intellectual case for God in their lives, but you, you speak to their heart. I have seen you teach about God and preach and men are moved to tears, I gave you a ministry a year ago, with only you, Derrick, and Ernie as members. In one year you and God have increased that to over forty young men. That is special."

"Without your mentoring, I wouldn't have been able to do it, sir."

"I appreciate that, Nathan, but it is God that has given you that gift. I recognize that, not many ministers can move men like you can. Look at what you have done with Ernie. I preached to that young man for years and could never reach him. You come along and in a year you have helped him turn his life around, and that is remarkable."

"I know sir, but usually that conference holds about one thousand people, I have never spoken to that many people before, and I think that Jeremiah would be a better-"

"My decision is final, Nathan, now go and send my son in so I can let him know." Fisher said as he turned his back to Nate and ended the conversation.

Nate got up from the chair, returned to the table as he wondered about how and why Fisher was so short with him. He didn't want the assignment, but didn't want to disappoint Fisher. Later, he talked to me about it.

"I don't know what to do man, I ain't ready for an engagement like that, plus I don't know how Jeremiah is gonna take it," Nate said worried.

"Nate, Fisher thinks you can do it. I think you can do it, and so does Sandra. God will be there with and for you, you will see."

"I know all of that, man; it's just that I have to feel that I can do it. And I don't."

"Trust God, Nate, it will all work out."

Nate heard me, but he didn't believe it. When it came out that Fisher gave the engagement to Nate instead of Jeremiah, the congregation took sides. Some felt Nate was perfect for it, and others felt Fisher snubbed his son. It created a bit of a schism among the people, and there was plenty of talk and gossip until Fisher addressed it in a letter he sent out to most of the congregation. In short, he explained that he reserved the right to use the discretion that God afforded him to make decisions based on spiritual insightfulness and not the whims and opinions of men. Everyone got the message, and in the weeks leading up to the conference things started to quiet down.

Jeremiah took things relatively well, he had recently gotten married also, and between the church business and his new wife, he didn't have the time to devote to the conference anyway. Nate worked night and day on his message. Sandra said he would stay up into the late hours studying and reading for it. Sandra had seen a quaint little house in Tinley Park that she wanted to purchase, but Linda and I had to do all the leg work with her, Nate never had time. This man spent all of his time at work, reading, preaching, and getting ready for that speaking engagement. He wanted desperately to not disappoint Rev. Fisher, but Sandra started to get a little angry that her new husband was never around. She would complain about it to Linda and me, but she refused to approach Nate with the matter. We both assured her that she was not alone, Linda complained that Ernie was never home either, and I told her that I couldn't remember the last time Nate and I spent some brotherly time together.

But it was what it was; we all loved him and let him do his thing, for now. The night before the conference he stayed in the house and worked on it all day, then went to talk to Rev. Fisher late in the evening.

"Well, how do you feel?" Rev. Fisher asked.

"Nervous, you sure you don't want to reconsider, sir?" Nate asked smiling.

"Not a chance! Let me tell you something, Nathan, sit down," Fisher said gesturing to the table.

"What is it, sir?" Nate asked curiously.

"There are gonna be some changes in the ministry coming soon, and I wanted to first make you aware of them. I didn't want you to get things misconstrued; I want you to work closely with Jeremiah on the future of the church."

"Ok, that's not a problem."

"Good. I am gonna ordain Jeremiah next week after the conference, and you soon after."

"Don't you think you are moving a little fast, Pastor?" Nate said smiling.

"No, God has told me I don't have much time left," Fisher said in deep reflection.

CHAPTER 12

The morning of the conference, Nate was ready. He had his notes, his sermon message and scripture references outlined and all. I had gotten up early to drive him to the convention center, and Ernie was supposed to bring Nate's briefcase a bit later. The conference was to start at nine in the morning, and Nate was scheduled to speak around eleven. He was allotted an hour or so, because the head of the convention wanted to break for lunch shortly after noon. Nate waited upstairs in the anteroom because he didn't want to see the crowd in case he got a case of the nerves. As the speakers started to arrive, each of them spoke to Nate and tried to offer some advice, trying to keep him calm. A few of the more seasoned older ministers didn't say much, they felt he may flub it, and ruin the spiritual flow of the day.

Rev. Fisher arrived shortly before Nate was to speak; I went outside to the main floor and ran into him and Jeremiah.

"Oh, I'm glad to see you, Pastor. Nate is expecting you, I'll show you the way to the anteroom-"

"Why? I am not gonna go see him. I want Nate to totally depend on the Lord today. He is gonna be a glorious minister but he must learn to trust in the Lord. If I go up there, he will start asking questions and looking for my approval and encouragement, he will be fine," Fisher said confidently.

"Besides, Nate is very prepared, he will do fine," Jeremiah said.

"Well, maybe. But a vote of confidence wouldn't hurt," I interjected.

Rev. Fisher nodded and asked one of the ushers where his seat was to be. I felt he was being a bit tough, and he should have been more thoughtful of what Nate might be going through. As the convention room filled near capacity, which was around six hundred, I started to look for Ernie. Ernie was supposed to bring Nate's briefcase with his message and everything in it. Nate was to go on in a half hour and Ernie was nowhere to be found.

"Where the hell is he?" Nate said anxiously.

"I don't know, Nate, relax, he will be here," I said trying to console him.

Then a minister walked into the room bringing in Sandra, Linda, and Ernie. But Ernie was without the briefcase!

"Ernie, where is the briefcase?" Nate asked.

"You don't have it?" Ernie asked.

"No man, you were supposed to bring it, remember?"

"I thought Derrick was supposed to bring it, I left it at the church on the counter near his room. I didn't know he was here with you already."

"Why didn't you call? You should have brought it anyway, man. What were you thinking?" Nate asked angrily.

"I'm sorry, Nate, I assumed-"

"Don't ever assume, man. I told you that!" Nate said yelling, as other ministers started to notice.

"Uh, don't worry, Nate, just take your bible out there. Do you remember your text, and some of what you wanted to say?" I asked.

"Man, I'm going out there to speak to hundreds of people, I can't go out there stumbling! I depended on you, man!" Nate said turning back to Ernie.

I could tell Ernie was embarrassed, Linda and Sandra tried to reason with Nate but he was becoming irate.

I immediately grabbed Nate's hand and began to pray, which seemed to calm him a bit.

"Ok Nate, we gotta go take our seats in the audience. Remember what Fisher said about trusting God. Do that, and things will work out fine," I said as we all started to walk toward the door.

"Man, how am I gonna-"

"In all thy ways acknowledge him and he will direct thy path," I said as we all walked out.

I was so nervous for him, I know what he was going through and hoped that God would help him; he wanted to do so well. When I got to the main floor, there where hundreds of people, and everyone was beginning to settle in. There where widescreen monitors at the corners of the stage and flowers that spread outward from the podium. Someone placed a couple of seats on the stage that were occupied by the event coordinator, and the master of ceremony. There were men everywhere from all walks of life, men of all races and social backgrounds, and when I saw all of them, I really became afraid for Nate. I wrote on a small piece of paper what had happened and had it passed to Rev. Fisher, hoping he would give me something to tell Nate. I saw him read it quietly and he folded the paper and placed it in his pocket and simply stared forward. He didn't even look down the row at me!

The event coordinator stood up and approached the podium. He talked briefly about how pleased he was with the turnout, and how God had really blessed this year and how much money was raised for the various charities from the workshops. Then he began to introduce Nate. He talked about how Rev. Fisher the usual speaker could not make do it this year due to illness. He instructed Fisher to stand and the crowd acknowledged him with a hearty applause. Rev. Fisher had been the convention speaker for seven years, and had always done a good job. He then began to talk about Nate.

"Rev. Fisher has left us in very capable hands, this young man has a word from God for us and we are all ready to eat from the table of the Lord. He is a young man that has worked tirelessly with young men, and has brought close to forty men to Christ this year alone! I have met him and I am excited about what he has to say to us today. He is a minister of the Gospel under Rev. Fisher and recently, a newlywed! Without further ado, let me present to some, and introduce to others, Minister Nathan Williams!" The coordinator stepped aside and held his hand out motioning Nate to the podium. Sandra, Linda, Ernie and I all clasped hands together as we waited with baited breath.

Nate walked out from the side of the stage and shook hands with the coordinator as everyone stood up to welcome him. I looked down the aisle at Rev. Fisher and he was standing and applauding grinning from ear to ear. I also noticed most of the congregation had arrived and was applauding him also. We all hoped and prayed for the best, as Nate sat his Bible down on the lectern, and motioned for everyone to take their seat. As I scanned the room, I noticed the odd white man from the car that used to stake out the church in the back of the room taking pictures, he was still wearing his dark sunglasses. I immediately became nervous and uneasy about the situation as Nate praised God and went into his speech.

****

The mafia member knocked at Nate's office door and made him aware that the man they had found was downstairs along with a nephew of his. They had been duck taped to a chair next to Al's mother and her grandson.

Nate walked down the narrow dank corridor to the area known as the dungeon, and adjusted the pistol in the small of his back. He was accompanied by members of Dana's regime. Everyone stood at attention and scurried around to look busy as Nate walked in.

"Alright get your shit together now," Nate said sternly.

There was a foul stench in the room, because the mafia members were instructed to not let the grandmother nor her grandson use the bathroom. They were told to "piss and shit" right where they sat!

Nate snatched the tape away from the man's mouth and started his interrogation.

"What's up, man, you know me?" Nate asked smiling.

The man shook his head nervously no, as sweat poured from his face with fear.

"You know that motherfucker Al, don't you? And don't lie to me!" Nate yelled.

The man shook his head "yes" nearly white with fear.

"Good, you know where he is? See, cause he took a lot of money from me and disappeared, I heard through the grapevine that you knew where he was and took some money from him. Is that true?" Nate asked smiling patronizingly.

"N-no sir, I don't know nothing about that stuff. I got some money from him before he left. But I don't know where he is," the man said trembling.

"I'll be damned, don't nobody know where this motherfucker is, Mike," Nate said condescendingly.

"How much did you take from him?" Nate asked him.

"I don't know about five thousand dollars, I guess."

"Who the fuck is he?" Nate asked motioning to the man taped and seated next to him.

"That's my nephew, what is this about?" the man asked.

"I'm asking the fucking question's nigga!" Nate shouted.

"Ok, I'm sorry," the man said humbly.

"Naw, you ain't bitch, but you gonna be! All of y'all gonna be!"

As Nate stood up, he noticed the grandmother starting to go to sleep, he took a glass of wine sitting on the table and splashed it into her face and slapped her twice across the face.

"Wake yo fat ass up, bitch! Ain't gonna be no sleepin in here. I want all you motherfuckers awake for when he get here!" Nate yelled.

Everyone burst into laughter in the room while the hostages shook with fear then Nate walked toward the door to leave. Before he left the room, he gave his final instructions.

"Alright, the same rules apply to these new motherfuckers, give these bitches just enough to eat to keep them from starving and nobody sleeps. Don't let any of them go nowhere, and all of them will piss and shit right where they sittin!" he said as he walked out and slammed the door.

■■■

"My name is Nathan Williams; I am a walking, breathing miracle of God. I am evidence that God can do anything! Just five years ago I was an animal, a killer, a drug dealer, and a parasite of society at large. I had a hideout not far from this convention center. I sold crack cocaine, heroin, powder cocaine, and any other drug that would yield me a profit. I had a love affair with lawlessness, an addiction to hate, and a fetish for mayhem. I was mad at the world, God, and life in general. I was worth nearly eight million dollars, but I was poor in spirit. I owned the best clothes money could buy, but I was naked of honor and integrity. If one of you had seen me back then, you probably would have went out of your way to cross the street or avoid me at all costs as well you probably should have. Back then, I would have killed anyone of you like a fly, and sleep like a baby that same night.

Then I lost it all. I lost my family, my so-called friends, my money, and my will to live. I found out the hard way that materialism may have made me happy but it didn't give me joy. I found out that although I was surrounded by people, I was very lonely. I found out that the best things that life had to offer, money couldn't buy. The Bible asks the question, what does it profit a man to gain the world but lose his own soul? I had found out the answer was...nothing. If it had not been for God and my brother, I would surely be dead.

God blessed me to come here today to help someone, help someone understand that the wages of sin is death, but not a death of the physical, but a mental, spiritual, and emotional death, a death of epic proportions, a death that affords a man no peace. I say to you today, my friend, nothing in this world is worth that, nothing in this world is worth eternal separation from God. So as I stand here, I liken myself to Paul the Apostle having been blinded on the Damascus road, I stand here today making the promise that henceforth nothing shall separate me from the love of God, neither death nor life, nor angels, nor principalities, nor powers, nor things present, nor things to come, nor height, nor depth, nor any other creature, shall be able to separate me from the love of God, which is in Christ Jesus, our Lord......"

Nate spoke so smoothly and eloquently. He went on to talk of his experiences helping others to find God, and by the time he finished, there wasn't a dry eye in the place, he received a standing ovation as we all stood up and gave glory to God for what he had done in his life and the miracles that God had performed in others through Nate. That day, over six hundred people, mostly men, wept and cheered after hearing Nate's message. I had never been more proud of him. I peeked down at Rev. Fisher and he was standing up cheering wiping tears from his eyes. The coordinator grabbed him and hugged him with tears in his eyes also. Ernie leaned over and whispered loudly to me that he believed God made him forget that briefcase. I completely agreed, I was moved more than everyone in the house because I was there, I saw the beatings, the drugs, the brutality, and carnage. I witnessed firsthand how far God had brought Nate. I looked back to see if the man with the camera was still there and noticed that he had left.

Later that night, we all went out for dinner and discussed the day's events. We all poured over Nate and talked about how well God used him earlier. We ate and drank most of the evening. Nate received at least ten speaking engagements later that day. As we all sat around the table talking and laughing, Sandra stood up to make an announcement.

"Everyone, I would like your attention please," she said as she tapped her fork against her glass. Everyone sat up and gave her the attention she solicited.

"I would first like to thank God for the remarkable job my husband did today as we all know."

Everyone agreed and cheered, as Nate smiled and tried to stay humble.

"I am so proud of him as we all are. I just hope that his twins feel the same way!"

We all were so shocked and amazed and Nate sat up in his seat and dove for Sandra over three of us! Everyone cheered and gave all of the congratulatory hugs. We were all surprised because Sandra had been told by many doctors, years before, that she was unable to have children, so to hear that she was having twins was a true miracle. It was one of the greatest moments for us all, and it would be the last great moment for some time to come.

CHAPTER 13

Over the next few months, Nate spent time speaking at churches all over the community. Almost all of them loved his approach to speaking and ministering. He would spend a lot of time going door to door, hanging out in front of men's clubs, liquor stores. Anywhere men hung out, sooner or later Nate or one of the brothers in the ministry would be there. Ernie turned out to be a big help to Nate, keeping the guys in line and helping Nate with his speaking engagements and watching out for Sandra through her pregnancy. I rarely saw Nate, I was getting close to finals and I had to study most of the time. Every now and then I would see our mystery friend sitting outside of the church or one of the areas where Nate would evangelize. He never approached Nate, which was odd, he would only take pictures write down notes and drive away. After being afraid of him for so long, Nate and I started to find him amusing.

The only time I ever saw Nate relaxing was when he would be studying, talking to Fisher, or watching the White Sox. He never lost his passion for them, and often talked about going to a game one day, which I always told him was too dangerous. All was good, Nate spoke and guys came to Christ without hesitation. They all loved him, Nate always had a leadership quality about him. Guys just wanted to follow him and believed what he said.

"You know, Derrick, I should have done this years ago. I feel like I wasted half of my life," he said reflecting.

"Everything is done on God's time, remember?"

"True, you got a test or something tomorrow?" he asked as he stretched.

"Nah, probably will relax. It's been a while since I have been able to."

"I was hoping we could hang out, you know, make a day of it, it's been a while since we hung out, don't you think?"

I had been noticing it for about eight months; I was shocked that he did.

"What you got planned?"

"You'll see. Sandy's gonna hang out with Linda and do some shopping and all's well at the church, so we are clear."

"Ok, fine by me."

I was so happy about hanging out with him I could hardly sleep, there was so much I wanted to ask him and talk about. I just didn't want bring back the past, he had so much going on and I didn't want to infringe on that.

The next day we started out early, we went out to breakfast and drove around Joliet wasting time talking.

"You know, Derrick, we are going to Chicago today," he said while driving.

"Whoa, Nate, I don't know about that. I know we have different lives now and all but it hasn't been that long. It's still too dangerous for us out there, you know?"

"Derrick, whatever will happen will happen. I want to go visit the cemetery, and go to a Sox game. It's 2004, I'm tired of being afraid all the time, life is good. I just wanna enjoy it, that's all."

I didn't argue, I could tell it wouldn't have done any good anyway. We went to the cemetery, visited our mom's and the graves of Mike, Dana, and the others. We talked and laughed about old times, and headed to the game. It was the first time Nate had been to a Sox game in ages, he had a great time. Boy did we laugh and reflect, all the crazy times, even some of the bad things we had done.

"How come it took us so long to do this?" I asked during the seventh inning stretch.

"We both have been so busy; sometime we just get caught up in the rut of life you know? I am so happy now, Derrick, it seems like I can finally exhale. But you know what? I am exhausted."

"I bet you are. When do you ever take a break?"

"It's not that, I haven't had a good night's sleep in over a year."

"Why not?"

"Those poison dreams, I can't seem to shake them."

"Oh, have you told Fisher about them?"

"What can he do? I think it's my conscience, man. I have done a lot of wicked things, Derrick."

"Really, no you haven't," I said jokingly.

"No really, Derrick, I am having a hard time dealing with it. I mean I can understand all the other attributes about God, but his forgiving me that's the one I can't understand."

"Well he has Nate, but seems that you haven't forgiven yourself, you've got to do that, and then you will be able to move on."

"I guess you are right, I just feel that I should be punished or something. I don't know."

"Let it go, Nate, Jesus paid it all, and all to him we owe. That's what is remarkable about this thing called salvation, Nate. He paid the debt of our sin and now we go free in the Lord."

Nate never responded; he just kind of stared off into space. After the ballgame that the Sox won I might add, we were on our way back to Joliet when we got a call from the church.

"Hey Nate, it's Deacon Jackson. They found Rev. Fisher unresponsive in his bedroom and they are rushing him to the hospital!"

"Oh Lord, which way do I go? How do I get there from here?"

"I'll show you, Deacon call Sandra and Linda and let them know what's going on."

We were worried that this may be it. Rev. Fisher had been having trouble breathing lately and we all took turns watching over him. His spirits had been improving, so we were optimistic. When we arrived, most of the congregation was there waiting outside and talking. Jeremiah and his wife were in the intensive care unit with him so we waited until they came out. According to Jackson, one of the deacons was sitting in the room with him when he stopped breathing; he quickly performed CPR and called 911. When the paramedics arrived they were able to get him breathing again but his breathing was shallow and labored.

When Jeremiah came out, his face was glossy, and he had been crying, he motioned for Nate to come to him.

"He asked for you, he wants to see you alone."

"How is he, what did he say?"

"I just told you, he wants to see you."

Nate confessed later that it was the longest walk in recent memory.

"Sir, can you hear me?" Nate asked softly.

"Yes, come closer, Nathan."

"Yes, what is it, sir?"

"I am so proud of you, son. I want you to be the best minister and father you can be, understand?"

"I will, I can count on you to be there to counsel me through it."

"No I won't son, not physically anyway. Help Jerry with the church for me, will you? I think you and him together can build a fine ministry," he said weakly.

"Ok, I will."

"Remember Nathan, the devil is your adversary and will try all he can to trip you up along the way. Stay close to the Lord, he will never leave you nor forsake you, understand?"

"Yes sir."

Nate said, after that Fisher fell asleep, we all stayed at the hospital until they asked us to leave. As we drove home, Nate reflected on his time with Fisher.

"That man was more of a father to me than I can remember anyone else being, he taught me so much."

"We are all praying for him and the future of the church. Rev. Fisher has touched so many lives," Linda said.

We all agreed that the church would not be the same without him, but for all intents and purposes, Rev. Fisher was gone. Even if he didn't die, he would no longer be able to lead us as a congregation. The transition of power had already begun, Jeremiah was beginning to give the messages on Sundays and Rev. Fisher was counseling him as he went along. We all supported his decision to anoint his son to lead the ministry, but no two leaders are the same. We tried to sleep that night but many of us were not successful. Then about seven thirty in the morning I got the dreaded call.

"He's gone, Derrick," Nate said over the phone solemnly.

"How long ago?"

"About an hour. Get dressed I'm coming over to pick you up. Jeremiah wants us to go over and fill out some paperwork and take care of the appropriate business."

"He can't do it?"

"He says he is not able to, you understand?"

"Yeah I guess so."

"Good then, you can explain it to me cause I don't."

Nate felt like that was a job Jeremiah should have done, in the recent year or so. Since he returned from the seminary, we noticed that he and Fisher were not as close. Many of us brushed it off, and refused to delve into it because it might start rumors. Sandra said that Jeremiah had already lost his mother, and now had to come to the realization that he was gonna also lose his father. Maybe distance from his father was his way of slowly letting go. She and Linda believed that to be the case, but Nate, Ernie and I didn't. We felt that Jeremiah had big plans for his father's ministry, and got back in town, rolled his sleeves and began working. That's not to say he didn't love his father at all, Fisher just wasn't one of his top priorities. Hell, Nate spent more time with him in that last year than Jeremiah did.

After stopping for coffee, we phoned the funeral parlor and arranged for them to pick up the body. We arrived at the hospital, signed the appropriate papers and Nate asked to see the body.

"Nate, are you sure-"

"Yes I am and I don't want to be talked out of it, Derrick."

With that, I didn't say anymore, I refused to go in, I wanted to remember him the way I last saw him. I never liked the last picture I have of someone to be laying in a casket. Nate wanted to say his personal goodbye to a man that was more of a father to him than anyone else he had known. Once we were all done, we left the hospital and informed Jeremiah that our end was complete. Jeremiah and his wife did all of the planning for Fisher's home going service. And when the day came, it was a splendid event. There were at least 5 choirs, along with our own, they sung beautifully. There were dignitaries, local and even state politicians who attended, and a plethora of ministers.

It was a very joyous service, an old friend of Fisher's performed the eulogy and we all agreed that he did a magnificent job. Rev. Fisher always taught that each life touches so many others, and that we live our funerals every day. He taught us to be careful of our daily interactions with people, because chances are we would run into that person again. He gave us so many life lessons, so many pearls of wisdom that I cannot remember them all. He was going to be missed by many; the date was October 15th 2004.

CHAPTER 14

2005

The year two thousand-five promised to be a fine year. By the end of January, most of us had begun to heal from the emotional loss of Rev. Fisher and look to a new and brighter future for the church. Jeremiah had already instituted many new changes, which enhanced the membership almost immediately. Nate and Sandra were enjoying their new daughters along with the growth and success of the men's ministry. Linda and Ernie had a newfound sense of purpose in their marriage; they seemed to have fallen in love all over again, for which they constantly thanked Nate. I was not far from graduating from the junior college with my Associate's degree in nursing, and it had been months since Nate and I had seen our guy in the car watching us.

Everything seemed to be peaches and cream so to speak, the only thing that worried me was Nate. Outside of enjoying the twins, he seemed to always be on the edge. He worked tirelessly with the ministry; writing sermons, speaking at various local churches, and studying the Bible. There was hardly ever time for himself, moreover, his poison dreams had seemed to kick into high gear.

"Derrick, I am so tired I want to fall out most of the time," he said as he flopped into the chair at his home.

"Have you taken anything?" I asked.

"Not really, I don't wanna be like some people who have to take a pill to sleep, and then a pill to wake up."

"What is it exactly that keeps you from sleeping? Is it solely the dreams?"

"Of course, and the fact that I can't seem to shut my brain off. Sandy tries to get me to take a sleeping aid from time to time and I do, I just don't want to get addicted."

"They are not all addictive, Nate, are the dreams still the same?"

"Yeah, they are horrible! Sometime I dream I am falling, or people are after me to kill me. I have dreams of Dana and Mike dead, babies mangled and dead trying to reach out for me. I'm tired of waking up in a cold sweat all the time," he lamented.

"Have you tried praying, Nate, asking God to give you peace of mind?"

"Derrick, I did that months ago, He has not answered my prayers."

"Personally, I think you should try the sleeping aids and maybe see a doctor."

"I've got some dates coming up soon, that I am thinking about canceling."

"Well, I will talk to some of the nursing students I know and see what we can come up with for you. Have you talked to Jeremiah yet?"

"No I have a meeting with him tomorrow about the budget for the ministry. I swear between you and I, I don't like the changes he has been making around the church."

"Well, why not? People are joining; everyone seems to be pretty happy."

"That's just it, people are joining, but are they changing? I am concerned with I have seen lately with some of these newer members. Take the Collins family for instance. I happen to know for a fact that he and his wife are still drinking and having parties at their home. Some of the attendees are other church members, and Jeremiah has Mr. Collins on the advisory board, that's not right. And the young girl, Selica, she is president of the choir, and she is shacking with a guy, Jeremiah knows these things, because some of the deacons have discussed it with him, namely Jackson."

"Nate, I wouldn't touch that if I were you."

"I'm not, I am just talking to you about it, that's all."

"Ok, cause like it or not Jeremiah was left in charge. I know there are a lot of people around the church who take issue with his decisions, but it's not our place you know."

"Derrick, I understand all that you are saying, I am just pointing out that there are questionable, ethical things going on and I am deeply concerned."

I didn't say anything, I knew there were pockets of people who didn't agree with the path that the church was taking, and I knew Sandy, Nate, Linda, and Ernie were among these people. I knew that there were people around the church that felt Nate would have been a better choice, but Rev. Fisher made his choice and as far as I was concerned that decision was sufficient. The church was taking a different direction so to speak, and whenever that happens people were bound to be unhappy. Jeremiah being younger was a bit more contemporary, and that bristled many of the congregants. Some began to leave, but they were replaced with newer people. It seemed that for every five or so that left, they were replaced with ten to twelve.

Jeremiah changed the landscape of the services, instead of letting the deacons open service, he instituted a "praise group". He hired a new minister of music, and changed many of the signature songs that were usually sung on Sunday service and moved to more contemporary gospel music. He ended many of the "Annual Days" that were a staple at the church since its inception, and began different projects like the Pastors Anniversary, Praise Central, The Praise Dance Team, Gospel Drill Team and others. These new additions were a bit too contemporary to some, they were fine with me, and that's where Nate and I differed.

Many of the budgets for the old ministries were being reduced not to say outright cut, and the men's ministry was not going to be any different. Nate and Ernie were extremely successful in their efforts and many men were coming to Christ, but the rest of the congregation felt changes needed to be made. They felt many of the tactics that were being used by Nate and Ernie were outdated, and the ministry needed to "catch up" with the ebb and flow of the rest of the church. Jeremiah agreed, and that was going to be a backdrop for the rift between the two of them. Jeremiah needed to talk to Nate, but first he felt he should talk with me, to maybe get a feel for how Nate might react.

"Hello, you busy Jerry? You needed to see me?" I said gently knocking on his office door.

"Yes, Derrick, come in please," Jeremiah said closing his Bible.

"I like what you've done with the office; I have always loved Cherry wood furniture."

Jeremiah sat back in his chair and adjusted himself carefully finding the words to talk to me about Nate. He always spoke with caution.

"Derrick, tell me, how do you feel about some of the changes that I have made in the church?"

"I think you have done a fine job. We have many new members, attendance at Sunday service and Bible Class are way up, and the new programs you have instituted are doing quite well."

"I know, and thank you for acknowledging that, but you didn't answer my question."

"I don't know what you mean?"

He got up from his chair, removed his top coat, adjusted his tie, and gave me the same eye to eye look that his father had given me many times.

"Just because an apple is good for you doesn't mean you have to like the way it tastes. A significant number of people here at the church admit the new changes have helped the ministry, but they don't approve of the methods. Some of these people were instrumental in helping my father build this ministry to what it is today, and I am eternally grateful. However, they want things to remain the same, and they cannot. Change is a part of life, Derrick, we all know that, and if this ministry is going to be successful, we must be opened to change, all of us!" He said instructively.

"What exactly are you driving at Jerry?"

"Nathan is one of my biggest and most vocal opponents here, Derrick. He believes that I am destroying my father's legacy with all of the changes that I have made, am I right?"

"Jerry I don't think-"

"Derrick, don't do that. You know I am right, don't you?"

"I know you two need to talk," I resigned.

"I know, and we will tonight. But I wanted to share with you some of the changes that I want to make to the men's ministry," he said reaching into his desk drawer and pulling out a lengthy pamphlet and placing it on the desk in front of me.

I looked at the pamphlet and thumbed through a few of the pages and closed it.

"I think not, Jerry," I said pushing it back toward him.

He folded his arms and gave me a puzzled look before he spoke.

"Why? I felt like if I included you that-"

"No you didn't Jerry, you wanted to sell me on this so I could help you sell it to Nate, and I won't do that."

He pursed his lips, took in a deep breath and exhaled.

"You are right Jerry, I am fully aware of the tension between the two of you. And to be honest, I know you have some good points, and so does he. I support you fully, because your father asked me to, but I won't side with you against my brother."

"I'm not asking you to take sides I-"

"It doesn't matter to me. You are gonna have to face Nate without my interference, that's the way your father would have wanted me to handle this. I will be praying for you both, now I gotta go study. Is there anything else?"

"No, Derrick, I believe that is all," he said reluctantly.

I got up from my seat and walked toward the door before he stopped me.

"Derrick, I am proud of you. No matter what happens I want you to know that."

"I know Jerry," I said before I walked out of the door.

Part of me wanted to warn Nate about his upcoming meeting with Jeremiah, but my better judgment told me not to. Besides, Nate was more than capable of handling things himself. Jeremiah decided to turn the meeting into a dinner, to which he invited me, Nate, Sandra, Linda and Ernie. He felt that breaking bread together might help ease tension and control angst. On the surface, things were supposed to go smooth with minimal shop talk. We were to keep things simple and festive. But the whole purpose of Jeremiah having the dinner was to talk to Nate so…….

"I'm glad you all came, I am so happy we could spend this time together," Jeremiah said smiling as he sat at the table.

We all gave our approval and sat down, as we prepared to eat. We were going to dine on roast this evening, and that happened to be one of my favorites. As we prepared to give thanks, Nate nudged me so that I would notice the "servants" preparing to bring the food in. Midway through the meal, the conversation started.

"Nate, I have received a formal invitation for you to speak at St. Luke church this weekend at their annual family day, did you have anything planned?"

"No, I received a call a couple of days ago. Is that the one in Chicago?"

"Yes, off 71st street. I figured that you grew up in that area and you would be happy to speak there. I accepted on your behalf, I hope you don't mind," Jerry said appealingly.

Nate and I looked at each other in a spirit of caution, Nate and I knew that going to Chicago would be dangerous for us, but Nate was not one to turn down any speaking engagements.

"No, that will be ok. Just for the next time, please let me know, ok Jerry?" Nate said without looking up from his plate.

"Oh, sorry Nate I just figured that-"

"It doesn't matter, Jerry, it's done, ok?" Nate said this time with agitation.

Then a sense of uneasiness crept into the room as everyone fidgeted slightly. Jerry tilted his head at Nate, placed his fork and knife down from his hands, wiped his mouth and spoke.

"Nathan, do you have a problem with what I did?" Jeremiah said with a sly grin.

"As a matter of fact I do, Jerry; I feel it would have been more appropriate for the pastor over there to call me first," Nate said looking Jeremiah square in the eye.

"I understand that, but some of us like to follow proper protocol, Nathan, I wish you would understand that sometime," Jeremiah said dismissively.

"What is that supposed to mean?" Nate asked.

"Boy, these potatoes are just right, they almost melt in your mouth," Sandra said trying in vain to change the subject.

"It means that I am the pastor here, Nathan, and it is proper protocol to talk to me before talking to one of the associate ministers for a speaking engagement."

"Your father never did things that way," Nate snapped back.

"You are right, Nathan, but that is the exact thing some people cannot begin to understand that my father is no longer the pastor here, I am! And no two leaders are alike," Jeremiah said combatively.

"We all know that to be the truth, Jerry, you can believe that," Nate said through clinched teeth.

With that Jeremiah popped up from his chair, now visibly angered.

"Nathan, you are to respect the office of the pastor, even if you do not care for his methods!"

"You know man, you don't get the respect your father did, cause you ain't the leader he was! You're running this church like it's a business, instead of the house of the Lord."

"Don't question my integrity; I was hip deep in the word of God when you were hustling the streets, man!" Jeremiah said angrily.

"Yeah? And now you're the one hustling, Jerry!"

"Go to Hell!" Jerry shouted as he pushed away from the table.

"It's the truth, Jerry, you will do anything to get butts in the seats everyone knows it!" Nate shouted also.

"And I suppose you have better spiritual insight on how things should be done?" Jerry asked Nate incredulously.

"Please you guys, let's not argue, you both have good points, let's just reason together and-" Sandra said before Nate cut her off.

"No sweetie, we have a different philosophy. Jerry here is trying to build a church, and I am trying to build people. I can't do this anymore, Jerry, I resign. Thank you for the dinner, but I ain't hungry anymore," Nate said wiping his mouth and starting for the door. I got up trying to control the situation as Jeremiah followed Nate continuing his harangue.

"Your resignation is not accepted, Nathan, you have a job here, don't be a quitter," Jerry said challenging Nate.

"I ain't a quitter, man, I can still do my work for God, I just don't have to do it here," Nate said putting on his jacket.

"Nathan, wait a minute, let's talk this over. Rev. Fisher wanted you two to work together, this is of the devil and you know it," Sandra said pleading.

"No it's not, baby, Jerry and I are just going down different paths. And this is something Rev. Fisher didn't foresee."

With that, Nate walked out of the door, Linda and Ernie gave Jeremiah a hug and thanked him for the dinner and promised they would try to talk to Nate. I was the last to walk out. There was something I had to tell Jerry, though. Something I noticed during his disagreement with Nate.

"Jerry, I noticed that you and Nate could never work well together. Simply because you both suffer from the same disease…pride."

Over the next few weeks we all tried to reason with Jeremiah and Nate, but both were too bullheaded to listen to reason. Nate gave his formal resignation to the board of deacons and trustees, and despite his promises not to, Jeremiah let him go. Nate's departure left an awful split in the church, many of the men left to follow him despite Nate encouraging them to stay and help Jerry. Nate rented a small storefront in the community and he and Sandra began their men's ministry. Linda and Ernie left the church also, and helped Nate and Sandra; I, on the other hand decided to stay. As a result, Nate didn't speak to me for a month or more , but we eventually set aside our differences.

Nate and the men called themselves the Mighty Men of Valor, and set out to save men throughout Joliet. Nate was enormously successful, and the men all around the city adored him. He fed the hungry, clothed the naked, and even helped some find jobs in the community. God swelled Nate's ministry to close to a hundred men. These were men who were fed up with the politics and grandstanding of many of the churches in the community and hungered for real Christian leadership, and Nate and Ernie provided that.

Nate had received an invitation to speak at the Solid Rock Church in Chicago at their annual Men's day service. Solid Rock was a smaller church, located in the Park Manor area where Nate and I grew up. I must say I was apprehensive about Nate going there to speak, but things were going well, and we had not seen our guy in the car in months. The night before the engagement, Nate called me at the church and asked me to pick him up the next morning and have breakfast with the family before we headed out.

"I thought Ernie was driving you?" I asked curiously.

"I thought I would spend some time with you first, me, you, Sandy, and the girls, is that ok?" Nate said sarcastically.

"Of course, man, but-"

"Good, see you in the morning." With that, he hung up the phone.

The next morning when I arrived at the house Nate seemed tired, but festive. He later confessed to me that he had had the best sleep in months, if not a year. He said that if he didn't like Pastor Halbert so much he would have cancelled just to stay in the bed. Sandra made pancakes; we all ate and had a great time. The girls were their usual darling selves and Nate played and laughed with them heartily. Later on, Ernie and a few of the guys arrived; we all got into Ernie's truck and headed toward Chicago.

On the way there, Nate simply stared out of the window and didn't talk much, every once in a while he would smile to himself as he looked at all the people on the streets in the old neighborhood.

"Hey man, let me ask you a question?" he turned to me and said.

"What's up?"

"How come you didn't leave the church and come help me?"

"One reason and one reason only…..God didn't tell me to."

"Really? And since when did you start listening to God over me?" he said jokingly.

"Right at that moment," I replied smiling.

As we turned down Seventy-First Street, we could see the drunks and "hypes" staggering down the street. There were old women pushing carts, middle aged women stumbling down the avenues as zombies high on crack. It had been years since Nate and I had been to the old neighborhood, and to see this dejection was a grim reminder of a life that had been. Many of those men and women probably started their addictions on our dope, and it hurt to see it. As we stopped at a light, a woman who looked to be near our age came up to the window and asked us for a quarter. She wore her addiction on her face, the hard lines and bloodshot eyes revealed many sleepless nights that she had stalking the streets for crack.

Nate pulled out some pocket change and gave it to her, as we drove off, I could see a tear welding in his eye. All of those people were a reminder of what Nate had done to his people, and the guilt was hurting him. The long drive down Seventy-First Street was a stroll down the corridors of his life. As we pulled up in front of the church and got out of the car, an older woman noticed Nate and I. Mrs. Lucille Robinson from the old days, she was momma Williams' friend.

"Nate and Derrick, is that you two? My God from Zion, you boys have grown up to be such strong soldiers for the Lord. Your momma would be so proud of you!" she said excitedly.

We both thanked her and gave her a hug and a kiss; I must admit it was so good to see her. It was like seeing momma Williams. Nate and I cried because she and momma Williams were so close.

"So, you will be the one to give the message today?"

"Yes ma'am," Nate replied.

As it turned out, she was a longtime member of the church and expressed her anticipation to hear what God had given Nate to share with us. After exchanging our contact information we gave her a final hug and headed into the church.

****

As Nate and I sat in his office discussing money issues and possibly setting up shop in Detroit, I heard a commotion in the dock area where most of the cars were kept.

"Nate, what the hell is that?" I asked jumping from my seat.

Nate finished the last of his Cognac in a gulp and gave a sly smile, he knew what was about to transpire.

"Come with me, G, I wanna show you something," he said sliding his 9mm into his waist.

When I got into the front of the house, I witnessed a gruesome sight; Dana had apparently found Al, his wife and their children and had roughed them up and was now bringing them to Nate as instructed.

"Found their asses on the boarder to Wisconsin going into Minneapolis," Dana said proudly.

"Good work as usual, girl," Nate said smiling as he picked his teeth with a toothpick.

Al, his wife, and their children had been blindfolded and bound with their hands behind their backs. Dana had roughed up Al and his wife, but apparently had not harmed the children. Nate walked over to Al and snatched his blindfold off to talk to him.

"Remember me, motherfucker?" Nate said smiling.

"Nate, Nate I can explain.....please let me explain," Al said desperately.

"Dude, I wanna hear your story, don't worry. You can tell me whatever story you wanna tell me as long as at the end of that story you got my motherfuckin money," Nate said sarcastically.

Al looked down at the concrete in the driveway signaling that he didn't have Nate's money.

"Take their asses downstairs," Nate ordered.

"What about the kids?" Dana asked.

"Take them too, take them all."

"Nate, what are you doing? You promised that-

"Hey, hey hold on, G, I aint gonna hurt Al or his wife and kids. I promised you that and I intend to keep that promise. I'm just gonna scare him up some, teach him a lesson," Nate said still picking his teeth.

I was a bit relieved; I had figured Nate had given up his search for Al and his family. I had been out of town to Florida with Jon, and when I returned no one had said anything to Jon or I about what the family had been up to. Later I found out Nate had given strict instruction not to tell me anything, which pissed me off. I followed them all to the dungeon and saw a sight that made me want to vomit. Close to nine members of Al's extended family were lined up against the wall, bound and gagged. They hadn't eaten in days. Nate instructed to give them just enough to keep them from passing out; which consisted of cheese sandwiches and water. Al's mother had been gagged and bent over a chair beaten and raped by Dana's crew and appeared to be in a shell-shocked state. I thanked God Al had been blindfolded again so that he couldn't see the grisly sight.

"You animalistic son-of-a bitch, how the fuck could you do this?" I said through gritted teeth.

Nate shrugged his shoulders nonchalantly, as he threw a chip into his mouth.

"At least, take his family upstairs, Nate!" I said in a loud whisper.

Nate looked at me, pursed his lips and gave Dana the order to take the wife and children upstairs.

Nate gave Al some more duct tape around his wrists to reinforce his restraint, and snatched away his blindfold again. Al dropped to his knees at the sight and let out a yell so loud that everyone jumped. He crawled over to his mother and tried to talk to her with tears flowing down his face. The guilt of what he had done engulfed him and he cried for his mother to answer him, she just looked at him with a blank look on her face. I turned my back; I just couldn't watch anymore, the sight was just too emotional.

Al managed to sit on his behind and put his head in-between his knees and wept like a child. I snatched a blanket from the floor and covered Al's mother and glared at Nate. Al looked up from his pain and gave Nate the look of a wounded child.

"How man, how could you do this to my family, Nate, how? You really are a monster, how could you do this to an old woman, a woman that look just like your mother, how man just tell me how?" Al pleaded.

"Nigga, fuck you! I was good to you, I gave you a chance to help your sick daughter and you stole my money!" Nate shouted.

"And you violated and exploited my wife, man. You think I didn't know that?"

"Shut the fuck up, nigga! Where's my fucking money?"

"I don't have it, Nate, I spent most of it. Please let my mother go, do what you wanna do to me, but let my family go man," Al pleaded through tears and anguish.

"We got a problem here Al, a big problem. You see, I promised my brother here that I wouldn't hurt you and your wife and children. You don't have my money, and just letting you and your peeps walk out of here is how do you say…counter intuitive" Nate said smiling.

I looked at Nate and wondered how he was gonna handle this situation. He was right he couldn't just let them all go. He had to do something, so he made a fateful decision.

"Tell you what I'm gonna do, you took three hundred thou from me. Now I'd like to compare myself to the Italian boys, and they wouldn't let you take that kind of money from them and walk away. Somebody has to die, and if they can't kill the one who stole the money or their immediate family, they would take the next best thing," Nate said.

"Nate, don't do it!" I said through gritted teeth.

Nate took a 45 magnum from Dana and pumped two bullets into the old woman's head spattering her brains on the floor. We all looked on in horror as the old woman's body jerked and slumped lifelessly over the chair. Al screamed out in terror for his mother and curled up into the fetal position grunting and crying out, as Nate walked over to him, and bent down close to his ear.

"Even, Steven," Nate said smiling.

****

Nate accepted a glass of water from one of the church nurses, and thanked her for it. We small talked for a while, with Rev. Halbert and some of his associates before entering the sanctuary. We loved Rev. Halbert, everyone did; he was a tall jolly man with a giving heart. Aside from Rev. Fisher, Halbert was one of the only ministers Nate truly loved and respected. After we shared a few laughs and talked about Rev. Fisher and his coming up in the ministry with Halbert, we entered the sanctuary. As customary in most Baptist churches, announcements were made, prayers were solicited, and offerings were collected, then Nate was formally introduced to start his sermon.

"He looks great, doesn't he?" Ernie said gleefully.

"Yeah, for the first time in a while he looks relaxed," I agreed.

Nate who always said he wanted to leave an impact every time he preaches surely left one today. He gave a prayer, took a drink from a glass of lemonade and spoke......

"In the beginning was the Word, and the Word was with God, and the Word was God. The same was in the beginning with God. All things were made by him; and without him was not anything made that was made. In him was life; and the life was the light of men. And the light shineth in darkness and the darkness comprehended it not. We, my friends are a part of that darkness; many of us have been bewitched by this darkness. We have been taught by this darkness how to think, how to feel, how to judge, how to believe and unfortunately how to love. We have been influenced by this darkness that right is wrong, and wrong is right. The darkness I speak of is not the devil, it is not hell, it is the darkness of pride. Like it or not pride, is the driving force in many of our lives, pride tells us to refrain from embracing when the light of God tells us to embrace. Pride tells us to lie, when the light of God begs the truth, Pride tells us to speak evil of men when we should speak well. Reason being, pride is selfish, the word of God says; The fear of the Lord is to hate evil: pride, and arrogance and the evil way, and the forward mouth. Pride affects our outlook on the passions of life; our families, our jobs, every aspect of our lives even the way we look at money. Money in and of itself is not evil, but it is pride and love of it that makes it evil. Pride represents the evil side of money. The Bible teaches us that the love of money is the root of all evil. The love and pride of money makes men do evil things, I know for I was one of those evil men. The love of money gives us a false sense of security, when we have an abundance of it, it makes us proud, makes us feel important. We don't look to the light for that security, we look to the money and cares of this world........"

Nate went on to chronologically tell of the things momma Williams did for money and security, the evil things that he did for the sake of money and security. Nate's sermon was basically his life story, and he told it with eloquence, with sincerity, with passion, and due diligence. As he approached his ending he gave us a final warning......

"................And if I were to leave this world today, I would give our youth a stern warning. Beware of the pride of life, love everyone as you would wish to be loved, and most of all, be mindful of your attitude toward money and the spirit of gross materialism. Money definitely has its place, however be mindful that pride and money are a horrific mix. Money when placed in the hands of a spiritual steward, can accomplish much for the Lord, but the evil side of money is the common denominator that corrupts and destroys. May God bless you all."

Nate received a standing ovation from everyone. I stood because I watched him walk down life's avenue in that sermon, and it taught me a lot about his views on where he now stands and where he had been. Rev. Halbert gave him his customary bear hug of approval, as he and Nate came down from the pulpit. Everyone filed out of the sanctuary after the benediction to shake his hand and give him smiles and kisses of love. Ernie walked up to Nate and whispered into his ear that the White Sox game had not long started and they were down by five.

"You know I'm never gonna live to see this team make the World Series!" Nate said with slight disappointment.

"I don't think so, young man, they look pretty good this year," Rev Halbert said smiling.

"Hey Nate, Sandra is on the phone," I said handing it to him.

"Hey what's up honey?" Nate said smiling.

"Oh nothing I got two young ladies here that want to speak to you," Sandra said over the phone.

"Hello daddy!" The little voices screamed jubilantly.

Nate had a quick conversation with the girls as he beamed with pride and told them he loved them, Sandra told him to pick up some seasoning salt from the store on his way home. Nate agreed that he would and told her that he loved her and he would be home around two-thirty because he wanted to drive around the old neighborhood. A move I strongly disagreed with, but Nate talked me into doing it anyway. We all gathered outside and noticed that no one had left; nearly the whole congregation gathered outside the church to talk to Nate again and give their well-wishes.

The whole group hugged him and told them once again how proud they were of him, Ernie and I told him to wait there while we went to get the car, we were all on cloud nine. So much so that we didn't even see the gunman.

As Ernie and I walked away I felt a cold chill run up my spine and I turned around quickly to see a young woman lift up her hand and take aim at Nate, she fired two quick shots into his upper torso and I saw Nate drop his bible and clutch his chest as he began to fall backward.

I remember screaming his name and running toward him as fast as I could. Ernie followed behind me as the crowd wrestled with the assailant and tackled her to the ground. I remember shoving everyone aside crouching down and gently placing Nate's head on my lap as tears streamed down my face.

"Nate, just hold on ok. Call an ambulance somebody call an ambulance!" I screamed frantically.

Nate had a look of peace on his face as he spoke.

"I love you, Derrick, you know that?" he said

"Shh, don't talk Nate the ambulance is on its way. Just hold on," I said as I began to gently rock with his head cradled in my arm.

"Take care of Sandy and the kids for me, ok?" he said just above a whisper.

"Don't talk like that, Nate, now hold on, the ambulance is almost here. Call a fuckin ambulance!" I shouted.

"They are on their way," Ernie said shell-shocked.

I looked around to see that the crowd had subdued the young woman as everyone waited with baited breath to see what would happen next. The police and ambulance sirens became louder signaling that they were close.

I looked down at Nate and saw him looking up at the sky as his eyes rolled around he began to speak......

"The Lord is my sh-sheperd; I shall not want. He maketh me to lie down in gr-green pastures: he leadeth me beside the sti-still waters. He restoreth my soul: he leadeth me in the paths of right-righteousness for his name's sake.

Y-Yea, though I walk through the valley of the shadow of death, I will f-fear no evil: for thou art with me; thy rod and thy staff they comfort me.

Th-thou preparest a table before me in the presence of mine ene-enemies: thou anointest m-my head with oil; my c-cup runneth over.

Sh-sh-surely Goodness and mercy shall f-follow me all the days…of my life: and I will dwell in the house of the L-Lord for ever….." he said before he fainted.

The emergency medical personnel gently took Nate from me and placed him into the ambulance as I climbed in him. Ernie promised to follow the ambulance to wherever they were taking him. I watched those men work feverishly to save my brother on the way to the hospital. I wouldn't look at them, I prayed so hard to the Lord to save him. We arrived at St. Bernard Hospital and the men whisked Nate out and took him directly into the Emergency Room. I was instructed to wait in the waiting room, where I prayed even harder.

When Ernie arrived he asked me if there was any word yet and I told him no. He immediately got down on his knees and prayed with me. A doctor came in to tell us that they were taking him to emergency surgery. I instructed Ernie to call Sandra and tell her what happened and to come down immediately. Within an hour, that emergency room lobby was packed with people from Halbert's congregation. Jeremiah and his wife were there and we all prayed to God for Nate's recovery. I cried and prayed so much I became hoarse.

After an hour or so, I decided to quietly take an elevator upstairs to the surgery suite. I remembered from being there years ago that I know a guy who worked there, I prayed he was there so I could get some information on Nate. Upon getting off the elevator and walking toward the operating room suites, I ran into another person Nate and I knew years ago. We exchanged pleasantries and I informed him of my situation, after telling me how sorry he was, he went into the back and motioned for me to come with him. I quickly changed into the operating room bunny suit and shoe covers and cap and followed him. Just as I approached the room where they were working on Nate, I saw the doctor call for time.

I felt like someone had taken all the air from me, the doctor came out and my friend pleaded with him to let me into the room to say my final goodbye to my brother. The doctor reluctantly agreed. I walked into the room as the nurses and surgical techs were shutting down the various medical equipment. Many of them gave me an ominous look, as I walked toward Nate's body. I remember looking at him quickly and giving him a kiss on the forehead, I gently pulled his eyelids shut and pulled the sheets up around his neck and walked out of the room.

When I got downstairs, Sandra noticed me walking toward the crowd and ran up to me.

"Tell me Derrick, tell me," she said crying.

I didn't say anything I just stared in disappointment and sadness.

"Tell me, did they kill my husband?" she said now realizing it was over.

We both embraced each other and cried, everyone sobbed looking at us knowing the obvious. Nathan Williams died at approximately 3:45pm on May 25th 2005

Epilogue

To say that I remember the subsequent days after Nate's death would be a lie. I walked around in a fog. Ernie came back to me and gave me some info on Nate's killer. I thought she was just some angry person with a vendetta. I thought maybe she was a family member of someone that Nate had killed, God knows when over God knows what. Turns out I wasn't too far from right; the young woman was the granddaughter of an old lady Nate murdered over her son's drug debt. Police interrogation files said she was bipolar and suffered from schizophrenia. She said Nate had destroyed her family years ago when he murdered her grandmother. I vividly remember the incident. At least now my brother could get some peace from his past.

Thinking back now, I realize that that was all that was wrong with Nate, God had forgiven him, but Nate had not forgiven himself. I wasn't any help at all to Sandra and the kids; I sat around feeling sorry for myself. Ernie kicked in and took care of things, with Sandra and the girls; I mostly moped around and felt sorry for myself. Nate was all I had in the world and now my world was upside down. The funeral, I can remember, was good, I recall getting out of the limousine and seeing guys lined all the way down the block standing military style and saluting the car carrying the body as it approached the church. I remember sitting in the front row of the church as Gatlin's funeral personnel brought in the flag-draped coffin. Jeremiah had them drape the Christian flag over the coffin signaling that Nate was a soldier, a soldier in the army of the Lord. I remember very little else. Jeremiah gave a wonderful eulogy, and there was plenty of singing and joy at his home-going to be with the Lord.

As everyone came down for the last view of Nate's body, I remained in my seat, I wanted to remember him the way he was. Everyone filed by and wished me, Sandra, and the kids well. The children took it pretty bad, they were only four years old and they would have vague memories of Nate. The whole thing was just so damn sad! I was shocked to see that one of the people who came up to look on at the body was Heather, from back in the day.

"Heather," I said in a loud whisper.

"Hello, Derrick. I am so sorry about this, I heard from some of the people in the old neighborhood. I had to come pay my final respects, Nathan was my first love," she said with her eyes welled with tears.

"He would love to have known that," I said reflecting.

"He did know it," she said as she gave me a kiss and walked on to speak to Sandra and the kids.

And to tell the truth, that is all I remember of my brother's funeral, I didn't go to the cemetery, I wanted to say my goodbyes later, alone.

About a week later I graduated from Joliet Junior College with my degree in nursing, an event I had hoped Nate would be there to see. It wasn't the same without my brother. Sandra, Ernie, Linda and the kids where there, I cried during the entire ceremony. I had a meeting with Jeremiah about a week later and told him I intended to stay at the church and help out in any way I could. He expressed extreme regret that the last conversation he had with Nate was an argument. I remember Fisher always saying that we should give each other our flowers in life while we could still smell them. Jeremiah said some outstanding things about Nate at the funeral, but Nate was not here to hear them.

About a month or so after Nate was laid to rest, I felt I was ready to go to the cemetery. I stopped by and gave Sandra the suitcase I had stuffed with cash years ago and told her to do with it what she wanted. She was shocked to see all of that cash, I told her a little bit about it, kissed her and the kids and left. I was so shell-shocked and crazy that I took a cab all the way into Chicago from Joliet! I cried all the way there, I remember getting out of that cab and being temporarily taken back at how much money it cost. It was a warm summer day, there was a hush over my world, a quiet settling that was a long time coming. I recall feeling that nothing would ever be the same. I walked over to Nate's gravesite and noticed the beautiful headstone that Sandra and the church picked. There was a simple and to the point inscription......Nathan Williams October 7th 1967- May 25th 2005; loving father and husband.

I stooped down and said a prayer and asked God why, why would he take the only thing I had left in this world. But I didn't get an answer; I lay on the grass and talked to Nate for what seemed like an eternity. I told him how much I missed him and promised I would visit and talk to him from time to time. After I cried my eyes shut, I got up to walk away and was surprised to be motioned over to a man sitting on the bench near the gate of the cemetery. I walked over reluctantly and saw some more men in dark suits walking behind me and gathering behind the man standing. He was an elderly man looking to be in his mid to late seventies, with beautiful grey white hair he had brushed into a horrible comb over. I noticed that the guys that stood around him looked official, and had earpieces and grim stoned squared jaws, they looked menacing.

"Hello, Derrick, it's good to finally meet you," the man said in a Bostonian accent.

"Uh, I'm sorry do I know you?" I asked curiously.

"Well I could give you a phony name but it's not necessary anymore, just call me Mr. X." he said confidently.

"Well, Mr. X, I just visited my brother's gravesite and I really don't have time to-"

"Sit down Derrick," the man said cutting me off.

I saw that I was in no position to argue and I was interested in who this man was and what he had to say, so I sat.

"It's all over, Derrick, your time is done," the man said plainly.

"What are you talking about, sir?"

"You know what I mean, son, it's all over."

I stood there looking at him incredulously; I didn't know what the hell he was talking about.

"Wait a minute; you really don't know who I am, do you?"

"No, I really don't!"

The man looked up at one of his bodyguards and gave a sly grin.

"You and your brother worked for us for over 15 years."

"Doing what?"

"What do you think son, selling drugs."

"I don't know what you're talking-"

"Oh cut the crap boy, don't play the bopeep role with me. Who do you think financed you, protected you, and counseled you all those years?" the man said with authority.

"Are you the F.B.I?"

"Well, we like to consider ourselves a little more intelligent than that."

"The C.I.A."

The man smiled and wouldn't give an answer to my question, and went into his explanation.

"Ok son, obviously your brother kept you in the dark for a reason. Whatever that was between you and him, I represent the intelligence agency. You and your brother sold drugs for us in Chicago between 1985 and 1997, right up until you blew up that house in New Lenox."

"I knew it, I always knew it. You used my brother to sell drugs. You, Trent, and the Chicago police department. You used him to destroy the black community, that's all you sons of bitches do, go from black community to black community dumping drugs and killing people. Well it's gonna stop here I am going to the press with this, you can believe that-"

"No you won't, Derrick, no one will believe you. Anyway, you walk away now and you won't make it to the corner and you know it," the man said plainly.

"I'll tell Jon, I'll call him in prison cause he knows-"

"Jon, oh he's dead. Nasty accident, Derrick, but you know how it goes in prison anything can happen."

"That's it, he knew the truth and you killed him for it. He was gonna tell someone and you had him killed!" I said.

The man let out a hearty laugh and slapped his knee, as he lit a cigar with a very fancy lighter. After taking a puff, he began to explain.

"You black people; you kill me, you really do, always looking to point the finger at the white man, always looking for the great white conspiracy. Now, son, if you're done with your black power bullshit, I will tell you how things really happened.

In the 80's the agency worked along with the state department to try to get rid of some rogue figures in Latin America. We worked with the Contras, and some other guerrillas to bring stability to Latin America and help put in people and leaders who support Democratic interests. We found out that the only way to do this was covertly, simply because the Latin drug lords and cartels were too powerful, moreover we were out of our element. The problem was the Congress and Senate would never finance or ok, any covert action. We had some congressmen and low level military people in our pockets that would help us hide it, but they assured us that the finance was strictly our fence to climb.

We did our homework and found out that we had the military might to pull it off in close to five years, just before Reagan would be up for re-election. However, it would cost us nearly five million dollars a quarter! Now how do you come up with that kind of money to finance an illegal war without the proper authorities knowing about it? There was only one way ...drugs. Getting the drugs into the states would be easy; the challenge would be selling it and hiding it. Finding the right people to distribute it and take the fall if anything went wrong, we recruited some guys to do some selling in the Hollywood circles, you know? But powder cocaine was too expensive, and it wasn't yielding the profit we needed."

The old man went on.....

"All of a sudden a young man in Oakland came up with an idea on how to use the paste that was left over when cocaine was cooked down, they called it freebase. That did much better than the powder cocaine, so, we stretched out to the inner cities, and saturated the streets with freebase."

"Why the inner cities?" I asked.

"Because, Derrick, it's the easiest place in America to fist fuck, and not worry about town hall meetings, nonprofit organizations, the American Civil Liberties, and all of those fuckheads! You can drown the black community with drugs and make a huge profit without a lot of backlash and bullshit."

"What about the black leaders, surely they would give you some heat," I reasoned.

"Politics and money make strange bedfellows," he said with a sly grin.

"And you mean to tell me no one said anything?" I asked.

"Derrick, in the black community someone always seems to be looking the other way. Once we went into crack, the whole thing got enormous. We went from dealing with our people to needing once removed black people that would sell for us without really knowing who they were selling for. That's where your brother came in. We had large distributors in L.A, New York, the south, and in Florida. Chicago was untouched. Therefore, we needed a guy that would handle the entire city without getting picked up. We needed a guy that was street enough to handle the load, but smart enough and tough enough to death-lock the streets. Nathan Williams was the most cunning, cut throat, organized guys I had heard of, the only problem was he wasn't smart. That's where you came in. Nate was the brawn of the outfit and you were the brains we needed."

"That's a lie; I never knew anything about all of this!" I said standing up.

"C'mon Derrick, you may not have known the specifics, but you knew what you were doing." The old man retorted.

"You're lying, I didn't! I followed along but I didn't have anything to do with-"

"Whose idea was it to set intelligence so tight, to incorporate local police, ministers, local politicians, to have eyes and ears everywhere so Nathan could sell his drugs with minimal static, huh? Whose idea was it that set up the Jackson killing, whose idea was it to assist Jon in washing money all over the fucking county?"

"I was protecting my brother!" I yelled.

"And the house, whose idea was it to blow up the house killing over 25 people and hiding your brother, huh?

You stood by and watched your brother destroy an entire generation of people, so you could fit in and have a family! You are a bigger killer than Nathan, Derrick, you aided and abetted him in a mass genocide! Derrick, your brother committed those crimes because he loved money and he loved being somebody. You helped him because you wanted to belong!"

He was right, I could have walked away anytime I was ready, but I was a coward. All those killings, all of the heinous crimes I witnessed and never walked away. I cared about all of those people, it's just that I was more preoccupied with myself, my needs, my wants, my selfish desires, and my lack of self-esteem. I did a lot of talking in those days, but I never did anything to stop that madness. I flopped back down on the bench, having been shown for the first time what I really was. I was weak; I was a coward. I put my head in my hands and cried. The old man was right, it was wrong for them to dump drugs in our community to finance their illegal activity, but it was also wrong for us to use those drugs to destroy our people. That's the hard lesson many drug dealers don't understand, just because white people put vices in our community, it doesn't mean that we have to use those vices for our own selfish gain. Just like Nate had preached, it was the money, the pride, and the materialism that bewitched us.

I felt like scum, like I deserved to die, then again I wasn't so sure that wasn't about to happen.

"What now? You gonna kill me?" I asked.

"Kill you? No, I would like to, in fact not killing you is extremely counter intuitive. But I promised an old friend that I wouldn't harm you or your brother."

"Trent, he looked out for us, didn't he."

"Not exactly! You see, it was Trent that brought Nate to us."

"Why would he do that?   He cared about us, he loved momma Williams and promised-"

"To look out for you all right - Detective Trent was working for the agency for years. He groomed Nate for the job not long after his mother died. We needed someone and Trent gave us you two."

"But why?"

"Because we threatened to destroy him, that's why. We watched him carousing around for years with the Williams woman; you see it was either your asses or his."

And that explained why Nate hated Trent so much, Nate knew Trent sold him down the river and into a snake pit from which he would not escape alive.

"Nathan agreed to give us two million dollars a quarter, and everything worked out great until you boys got too cute. When you guys killed Jackson, we decided to pull the plug on the project. Trent pleaded for your lives to my superior, and I granted his wish. Our plan was to give you two a file and watch you, until that young girl killed your brother, and now all we have is you."

"So, what are you gonna do with me?"

"You are leaving the states, Derrick," the old man said pulling an itinerary from his underling.

"You are getting on a plane to Africa, never to return."

"You are kicking me out of my own country?"   I asked mockingly.

"You are kidding me, right?   Son, you have committed enough crimes to earn yourself death row. If what you did came out, your own people would have you killed. No, you are done. Your name will be changed and the last thirty-four years you have been here have been erased. There will be no record of you ever existing in this country."

"What about my brother's family how do I know you won't harm them?"

"Why would we, they had nothing to do with anything we just talked about, and Sandra Jackson's reputation in her community is impeccable."

"And what if I don't leave?" I asked nervously.

The man just looked at me, as if the answer was too obvious. I gently took the itinerary from him and stood up.

"As soon as I can grab some things I will-"

"No Derrick, now, there is a plane waiting for you to leave in an hour. These gentlemen will take you to the airport. And remember Derrick, you can never return to the United States. Don't ever try to correspond with anyone here; don't try to write any books under any pen names. And don't think that you can wait twenty years and try to return, or we will kill you," he said nonchalantly.

I wiped my face with my hand and took in a deep breath, gazed around the sky and the cemetery. This was my punishment, this was justice. I had enabled my brother to destroy men, and now the worm had turned. As I looked down the hill I could see Ernie looking at me as he drove around toward the exit discretely. I then knew that he knew, and would tell the others somehow. I gave half a smile, shook the old man's hand and got into the limo and started toward the airport with the clothes on my back, and a truckload of memories and regrets.

October, 2005

Here in Ghana, the sun is hot and so are the hopes and promise of many of the young children with dreams of America and "making it" there. I can't help but think of Nate and everyone every day, wondering how they are doing, wishing I could see the twins and Sandra, longing for one last conversation with my brother. I remember reading a piece from some poet once, it said, "Whenever you wanted to communicate with someone that had passed on, you should write them a letter. I had a short break working here at the hospital, I wasn't much for writing, and Nate was never much for reading letters. So I pulled a piece of paper and started with these lines:

Dear Nate,

Man do I miss you! I think of all the times we spent together as boys and realize that youth is priceless. I would give anything to go back, to change things but I can't, what is done is done. But I do want you to know that I loved you, even though I didn't show it the right way, I guess we were all just hurting inside.

I like it here in Ghana; the money Jon and I filtered here years ago sure has come in handy! I opened a small clinic here and it is helping many young children who do not have adequate health care. So you see, the money has been put to good use.

Kiss momma Williams for me, and tell her I miss her and thank her for me for everything. Give my momma a hug and tell her I will see her someday. Explain to them, Nate, that we didn't mean to disappoint them, we just lost our way.....

Your brother Derrick.

P.S. The White Sox won the World Series!

What is past is prologue......

Hoodfellas II
American Gangster

Chapter 1

Haiti's clear skies, warm sunshine and inviting winds offer the perfect accommodating situation to explore the country's natural splendor. It's undiscovered, pristine trails, and foothills present the best opportunity for a serene bike ride. An abundance of outdoor opportunities reside in the back mountains of this precious island. The effervescent mood of the people is welcoming and embracing. With plenty of open spaces and green pasture for miles to come, warm climate and plenty of fresh Caribbean air, it's inexcusable to spend too much time indoor on this wonderful island. All of this aura brought a new sense of being to Deon Campbell. He felt rejuvenated when he first arrived in Haiti.

Deon thought he had left his criminal and troubled past behind and was hoping to start anew in a place where nobody knew his name. The fresh Caribbean air hit his face the minute he stepped off the cruise ship, and he just knew that the lifestyle of the rich and infamous was calling his name. With enough money to buy part of the island, Deon wouldn't have any financial worries until his calling from God. On the drive to Jean Paul's mansion caravan-style with a Toyota Sequoia ahead of him with armed security men and another Land Cruiser jeep filled with additional armed security men behind the limousine, Deon's mind was free to think about how he would miss his best friends and buddies, Short Dawg and No neck while riding in the air conditioned, long stretch limousine with his new friend, Jean Paul, and his entourage. He wanted to exact revenge on Short Dawg and No Neck's murderers and he would spend as much money it would take to make sure their killers don't live to see another day.

"I see you're a serious man and you're serious about your business," Deon said to Jean Paul as he sipped on a bottle of water while Jean Paul sipped on cognac. "In this country, you have to be. Don't let all the armed security intimidate you, it's a way of life here in Haiti," Jean Paul told him. An additional limousine also followed with all the luggage and money that Deon had to carry to Haiti with him. One of Deon's men rode with the second limousine driver. Keeping his eyes on the prize was very important and Deon didn't hide the fact that he wanted to know where his money was at all times. "I can't help but notice the worried look on your face, your money is fine. I have some of the best security men that Haiti has to offer…" and before the words could escape Jean Paul's mouth, gunfire erupted and bullets were flying everywhere from both sides of the road. A group of men emerged with machine guns as they attempted to stop the caravan so they could rob the crew. Deon had been in battle before, but this shit was ten times more than he had ever seen and he didn't know if Jean Paul had set him up or if they were just being robbed. "This fucking Haitian posse bullshit again!" Jean Paul screamed out loud. "Don't worry about a thing. All the cars are bullet proof down to the tires, but we're gonna teach these bastards a lesson, so they'll never fuck with me again. In each of those little compartments next to the button to lock your door is a nickel plated 9 millimeter, you guys are free to take out as many of them as possible. Their lives are worth shit here," he told them. At the push of a button, Jean Paul opened his compartment and pulled out two loaded .45 Lugar's. He cracked opened his window, and aimed at the pedestrian robbers. The crew of almost 20 men stood no chance as Jean Paul and his men returned fire with high powered guns from the barricaded bullet proof windows of the vehicles. A raid in Vietnam wouldn't even compare to the massacre that went on for about 2 minutes. After all the men were down, Jean Paul got out of the car to make sure that none of them had any breath left in them. It was like a firing squad as his men went around unloading bullets in the bodies lying across the pavement, ensuring that every one of the robbers was dead! The last crawling survivor received two bullets in each knee and one to the head before revealing that he was part of the Haitian posse located in the slums of Cite Soleil, the most dangerous slum in Port-Au-Prince, Haiti.

Even the United Nations guards, who are sent to monitor the situation in Haiti, were too afraid to go into Cite Soleil. The Haitian police feared confrontation in the slums because they were always outgunned and very few officers who went against the gang lived to tell about it another day. Jean Paul had been a target ever since his arrival in Haiti because he never hid his lavish lifestyle. A brash former drug dealer who grew up in the States, and was deported back to his homeland some twenty years later, he was not accustomed to the Haitian lifestyle or Haitian culture. After arriving in Haiti, Jean Paul had to learn his culture all over again. Americans like to say they're hungry enough to go do something drastic to feed their family, but in Haiti, those people literally lived it. Forced to eat dirt cookies due to lack of food, money and other resources, these gang members were tired of being hungry and anybody who got in their paths will pay the price for a better life, or better yet, food.

Many Haitian immigrants left Haiti with the hopes to one day go back to their homeland to help with the financial, economical, social infrastructure as well as democratic leadership. However, many of them usually find that what they left behind some twenty to thirty years ago has changed to the worst Haiti that they have ever seen. Since the departure of Baby Doc, Haiti has taken a turn for the worst and the economic climate in Haiti has forced many of its delinquents to become criminals of the worst kinds. While in the United States poor families are offered food stamps, subsidized housing and other economic relief by the government; in Haiti, relief only comes in the form of money sent to those who have relatives who live abroad. Those without relatives abroad suffer the worst kind of inhumane treatment, hunger, malnourishment, social inadequacies and the worst health.

To top off an already problematic situation, many of the Haitian politicians are unconscionable thieves who look to fill their pockets while the country is in dire need of every imaginable resource possible, including, but not limited to jobs, healthcare, social programs, education, clean water, deforestation, land development, any kind of industry and so on. Many of the elected officials offer promises, but rarely deliver on the promises after taking office. Most of the time, they become puppets of the United States government and in turn, look for their own self-interest instead of the interest of the people. Deon had no idea what he was stepping into and on the surface it appeared as if he would lead a peaceful life in the first Black republic of the world.

There's a price to be paid for freedom and winning a war against Napoleon's super French army with machetes and pure heart of warriors, the Haitians are definitely paying a price for it now. A brief history on the country was given to Deon and his crew by Jean Paul while on their three-hour drive to Jacmel from Port-Au-Prince where Jean Paul resided. Deon learned how Haiti, known back then as the pearl of the Antilles, has lost its luster and every resource it used to own due to deforestation. Coffee, sugarcane, cocoa and mangos are just a few of the natural resources and national products that the country used to offer the world, but most of it has evaporated because the government has not provided any assistance to the people to help them become self-sufficient in farming and land development. Security is one of the major reasons why foreign companies stay out of Haiti, and the government is not doing anything to bring back those companies as well as tourism, which helped the country thrive under the leadership of dirty old Papa Doc.

It was disheartening to Deon and his crew as they watched little kids running wild on the street digging through piles of trash looking for food along with the wild pigs and dogs on the side of the roads. Their faces reeked of pain, loneliness, hunger, starvation, malnutrition and hopelessness. Most of Deon's roughneck crew members were teary eyed as they watched this for almost two hours during the drive before hitting the scenic part of Haiti. Undeterred by the events that took place in the capital a few hours earlier, Deon ordered the driver to pull over in the center of St. Marc to hand out hundred dollar bills to a group of hungry children. The whole crew took part in handing out the money to the children who looked like they hadn't eaten a good meal since birth. Cindy took it especially hard as she was the only woman amongst the crew and Jean Paul didn't hide the fact that the minority two percent of white people in Haiti and another ten percent of mullatoes and people of mixed heritage controlled the wealth of Haiti.

It was evident who the wealthy people in Haiti were as they drove around in their frosty Range Rovers, Land Cruisers and other big name SUV's with their windows up as they navigate through the ghetto to rape the people of their wealth during the day while they rest their heads in their mansion in the Hills at night. The children rejoiced as Deon and the crew gave them enough money that would probably last them a whole month and more, to feed themselves and their families. Jean Paul was happy to see that his new friends sympathized with the people of Haiti, but he cautioned for them not to allow their kindness to become a habit as it could be detrimental to their livelihood.

Sample chapter from Ignorant Souls
The Johnson Family

Buck Johnson grew up in Charleston, South Carolina in a small two-bedroom house on a farm that he shared with fourteen siblings. He dropped out of school in the sixth grade to help ease the financial burden on his mother. Buck Johnson was the fifth oldest of fifteen children and one of the most responsible kids of Bill Sr. and Fatima Johnson. At thirteen years old, Buck became the man of the house. His two older brothers didn't really care about the way their father treated them and their mother when the elder Johnson was alive. They left before Mr. Johnson beat the life out of them. His twin sisters ran away from the abuse when they were both sixteen years old. They married two brothers who moved them to Virginia to start a family. The elder Johnson was shot and killed, leaving his wife to raise eight younger children on her own. He was an habitual drinker who didn't know his limit. Bill Johnson Sr. was the meanest individual when he was sober and twice as mean when he was under the influence of alcohol.

Bill Johnson Jr., the eldest child of the Johnson couple, left home at the age of eighteen because he was tired of his father's abuse of his mother and the rest of the family. He didn't want to turn his back on his mother, but every time he urged her to leave, she would not leave his father. Bill Sr. worked hard during the day to provide for his family, but at night, it was a whole different story. A bottle of moonshine was his best friend and his wife was his doormat. Bill Sr. would force his wife to have sex against her will when he was drunk and he would get violent if she refused. The blows to Fatima's face were normalcy in that household. Every little argument ended up in a physical beating of his wife. He would get upset at her for getting pregnant so many times, but he had no idea how to pull out nor did he care.

Bill Sr. had beaten his wife so badly one night that Bill Jr., or BJ, as he was called by the family, had to intervene to save his mother. Bill Sr. knocked her unconscious because she told him she was too tired to have sex with him while she was pregnant. He told her, "No woman ain't never gonna say no to me when I wanna have me some. I be the one who pays for this house here and I be the man of the house." Mrs. Fatima Johnson could only cry and wished that her baby wasn't dead from all the pounding she suffered at her husband's hand. When BJ saw his father hurting his mother, he pushed him to the ground to get her away from him. While still in his drunken state, Bill Sr. told his son, BJ, to get out of his house and if he didn't leave he was gonna get his rifle and shoot him.

BJ cried as he packed his suitcase with the two dress shirts and pants that his mother had sewn for him. He begged his mother to leave with him, but she told him that she couldn't turn her back on her babies. Her other children were still young and very dependent on their mother, as she was the only nurturing person in their lives. Bill Sr. wouldn't have been able to care for those kids, anyway, because the only thing he knew other than drinking was farming, which he forced all his kids to do everyday when they got home from school. When BJ left, his mother gave him all the money that she had saved, which was ten dollars. He had his mind set on New York City, but ten dollars was very limited even in the 1940's.

BJ was the biggest dreamer of all the Johnson kids. He wanted to become a playwright since he was a child. He abhorred his father because his dad pulled him out of school after he completed eighth grade. BJ believed that his father had cut his dreams short because his father never went to school to learn to read. His father didn't like the fact that he couldn't read his own mail even though he called himself the man of the house. He used to also get upset when BJ would try and teach his mother how to read better. Bill Sr. didn't want anyone in his family to know more than he knew. He resented the fact that he had to work the field all his life. Fatima was happy to send her kids to school so they could have a better life than she did.

Bill Sr.'s resentment was just, at times. Having grown up in the field and saw nothing but maltreatment at the hands of his father, Earl, who was a former slave bamboozled by his former owner who tricked him into working for free for many years so he could attain his independence and a better life for his family. His father was beaten and disciplined for being lazy even when he spent twelve to fourteen hours on the field picking cotton, while the slave master sat on the porch drinking lemonade in the shade. Earl Johnson was proud and had integrity. He knew how hard he worked for that white man. He raised his son, Bill, to be a hard and proven worker so that no white man could ever call him lazy. When Earl had to discipline Bill, he knew no other way to deal with him, except for the old ways of the master. The whip that marked his back for many years became the whip that marked his children's backs. The forbiddance of an education was also a repeated cycle in Bill Sr.'s life, because his father would beat him and tell him that he had no right to be smarter than him. Bill Sr. just couldn't break the cycle with his own children.

After BJ left the house, his father continued to abuse his mother and the second oldest of their children, Gerald, who was about seventeen years old. Unlike BJ, Gerald was not afraid of his father. Every time his father would hit him he would stand there and take his punches like they meant nothing. However, whenever his dad would beat on his mother, he would go and run behind the house. He couldn't stand there and watch his father beat on his mom. One night Bill Sr. was so drunk, he started beating on his wife with a belt because he didn't like the food that she had cooked. Gerald and Buck forcefully tackled their father and pulled the belt away from him. Bill Sr. didn't even have enough strength to get up from the floor. He lay passed out on the floor through the night.

The next day when Bill Sr. woke out of his drunken state, he gave Buck and Gerald the beating of their lives. He beat them so badly that they couldn't go to school for days. While Buck was hysterically crying through the whole beating, Gerald stood there and stared at his father without shedding a tear. Bill Sr. thought his belt was the answer to everything. Some of his kids managed to escape being beaten by him everyday, but Buck and Gerald were under their father's radar. Bill Sr. would beat Buck if he didn't bring him a glass of water fast enough while he was in the field. Gerald had gotten used to the beatings and lost respect for his father very early in his life. Bill Sr. was only able to instill fear in Buck with his belt. Buck didn't like the violent feeling of that belt against his premature skin.

The twin girls, Annie Mae and Aretha had their share of beatings as well, but when two young men who were visiting from Virginia offered them a better life in exchange for their hands in marriage, their mother urged them to get married to get away from their father. At sixteen years old, they didn't need their parents' approval to go up to Virginia to get married. They ended up sharing a two-bedroom house with the two brothers who were also farmers. The two men were in their late twenties and they came down to South Carolina to visit some family members when they ran into the girls in town. They owned a small parcel of land that was left by their dad. They grew cotton and raised cows. It wasn't a luxurious life, but the men would go on to take great care of the two sisters. The two brothers eventually built another house on the land so they could each have their own homes.

Gerald loathed his father so much, not because of the beatings he suffered at his father's hand, but because of the maltreatment of his mother by him. Bill Sr. had driven his first and oldest son out of the house and Gerald appeared to have been following the same path as his brother. It was a matter of time before Gerald exploded, as his father was making the situation at home worse for him. The drunker Bill Sr. became the more he beat on his wife and all his children were growing tired of it.

Mrs. Fatima Johnson was a courageous woman to stay with that man for as long as she did. Fatima wanted to show her children strength and dedication and in the process she put up with her husband's abusive behavior. Even though she woke up every morning and put her best face on, it was easy to tell that Fatima was suffering and the pain was starting to take a toll on her. It was bad enough that she had gotten pregnant every other year for the last twenty years while she had been with her husband, but his added abuse was wearing her thin.

Fatima found out she was pregnant with another child a couple of days after he had beaten her to a pulp. When she revealed to him that she was pregnant again he told her that she was a good for nothing harlot who could only have babies, during one of his drunk episodes. Bill Sr.

was also angry with Fatima and accused her of getting pregnant even though they could hardly feed the children they already had, as if he had nothing to do with it. He smacked her across the face and she ended up hitting her head on the cabinet above the kitchen sink. She was left with a big gash on her forehead and bleeding profusely while her two young sons, Gerald and Buck watched. It was the last time that Bill Sr. would ever raise his hands to Fatima.

Gerald was filled with anger and hate as he stood there watching his father denigrate his mother. Something came over him as he went to the back room, grabbed his father's .45-caliber shotgun, and blasted him across the chest, sending his father's body flying up against the kitchen wall. With tears running down his face, Gerald cocked the gun back and continued to release a barrage of bullets into his father until the gun was empty. By the time Buck and his other siblings grabbed the gun from Gerald, his father was laying dead against the wall, still with an angry, mean look on his face.

Gerald had had enough of his father taking his stress out on the family. All he could say to his mother was that he was tired of him beating on her and the rest of the family. Gerald reacted harshly because of his harsh environment.

Mrs. Johnson was mad that her husband had brought one of her kids to the brink of destruction, but she also knew that Gerald was not to blame. With blood still pouring down her face from her open gash, she grabbed her son and held him tightly in her arms to console him.

A Sample Chapter from Stick N Move III

Prologue

"Damn it, Man!" Shukre cursed through clenched teeth. He was covered underneath a table that sat in the center of the room, crouched in a fetal position, trying to ward off fierce blows. But, each time the stick would connect; a bone would crack, shatter, or break, upon impact.

Earlier that day, while taking part in a routine devised by most of the inmates housed in the same pod he lived in, doing pull-ups, push-ups, and dips, he was called to the front desk where an officer awaited him.

The wrinkled expression on his face told of his annoyance, and it was visible to the C. O. as he stated, "What the fuck y'all want with me now?"

Wiping at sweat that managed to form on his forehead, Shukre didn't resist when the officer placed the cuffs around his wrist, escorting him down a long hallway.

Entering through a door that was used as a conference room for visiting attorneys, Shukre's face registered shock finding two men in suits standing with their backs to him. They were busy sifting through a thick file, presumably his.

"Take a seat, Mr. Herring," the shorter of the two expounded. He hadn't done as much as glanced over his shoulder before adding, "Or, should I call you, Shukre!"

Immediately, Shukre's trouble antenna went up as an internecine feeling crept over him. For seconds, he stared unblinkingly at the two massive figures, still not coming to a conclusion of where he knew them from, but it was something, a vibe he'd gotten the moment his name was mentioned, that something destructive was soon to follow.

Turning, eyeing the officer who'd escorted him to the room, Shukre mouthed, "Look, I didn't call for any lawyers so I'd appreciate it if you take me back to my cell."

The guard eyed the two men.

"That'll be all," the taller gentleman quipped. "We'll take it from here."

The loud thud of the door closing caused Shukre to jump. His instincts warned him something distressful was about to ensue as he watched the short man retrieve a stick . . . a solid steel policeman-like wand, from his side.

The man tapped the stick lightly against the palm of his hand. Eyeing Shukre, he opened his mouth.

"I'm only going to ask you these questions once."

This was the vibe . . . that vexatious feeling that came over Shukre earlier. It ws something he'd learned when he was just a boy, and now that he was in his early twenties, the built-in alarm worked just as it did in the past. Maybe even better.

The tone in which the words came relayed the seriousness of the situation. And even though an implication was made that Shukre, in fact, knew this man, Dalvin Fleming, he wasn't about to tell the men anything.

The men had done this type of work before many times. It was in their profession, to search for and recover information, or an individual. And, one thing they didn't like was, being deceived.

Before giving Shukre a chance to answer, the taller man chimed, "Mr. Herring, if you try and deceive us, we'll know. And believe me, the pain we will administer you won't be something you will like. So, let's make this simple and easy as possible."

Shukre pondered this thought. He realized the men had the upper hand. He was still in cuffs. And, besides that fact, he was quite sure he couldn't take both of the huge men. So, without hesitating, he said, "Honestly, I don't know where to find them. I mean, I've been locked up for the past three mon…"

The compulsion, in which the steel rod slashed through the air, left a whooshing sound in Shukre's ears. With no time to react, he watched the wand arc towards his body.

"Oww!" he screamed, crying out in pain. What the fuck you do that for?" he bowed over in tears trying his best to cradle the excruciating pain in his limp, throbbing, and swollen hand.

By this time, sweat beads formed on his forehead. As he leaned his torso over, anything to alleviate the discomfort, he trembled from fear.

"Second question."

Though Shukre could hear the man mumble something, his ear felt as if he was struck inside a can two hundred fifty feet below the ocean.

Everything was distorted.

In his mind, he wondered who these men really were. They didn't bother in the least to flash their credentials, or tell him who they worked for. But, one thing was certain as he whimpered form the pain in his wrist, which now was being constricted by the cuffs. Whoever they were getting their information from, the source was on point.

"The girl, Yasmina, where is she?"

The question wasn't answered fast enough as the wand caught Shukre on the other wrist. Another ear piercing scream, Shukre bowed over from pain.

"Look... muthafucka!" he grit his teeth trying to thwart the massive amount of pain he felt. I'ont know why y'all are questioning me about this shit. I had nothing to do with any fucking prison break."

As soon as the words left Shukre's mouth, the men eyed each other.

"He knows something!" the shorter man admonished. "I never mentioned anything about a prison break. I only asked about Dalvin, and the girl, Yasmina."

For what seem to Shukre like hours, which in fact were only minutes, he underwent a fierce and painful beating. His nose, both legs and arms, fingers, the sockets of his eyes, even his toes were broken or ruptured.

Despite the vicious assault administered to him, Shukre fought with all the volition his feeble and bruised body could muster as he uttered, "No matter how much you beat me, I'm still not telling you shit!"

The words, although not convincing to the ears of the two men towering over Shukre, held a lot of conviction. They'd witnessed this type of gutsy bravado before, and they both knew that by the end of the session, they would get the much needed information they'd come for.

The smaller man laughed. "Mr. Herring," he said, "You're strong but foolish, and it amazes me how some people choose to make unwise decisions at important times in their lives."

Shukre coughed. The grimace on his face told of how much pain he was in. Through a course of wheezing and labored breathing, he quipped, "I'll die before I turn on my friends."

The comment caused both men to chuckle, but as quickly as the sneer came, it was replaced by evil facial contortions.

"Killing you will be the easy part," the second man, the taller of the two reiterated. He added, "But having your family watch each other die a slow and painful death tends to be the more difficult part of my job." He dangled a photo in front of Shukre.

The snipe alone caused Shukre to shudder, but it was the look in the man's eyes that sent fear racing through him. A tear slid the length of Shukre's cheek. The realization that his life would end soon, coupled with the fact that his body had past the point of numbness, Shukre tried holding onto the one place that still held a trace of sensation, his heart.

Curling his lips, he smiled at fond memories he'd shared with both, his family, and Dalvin. But, he also knew in giving these people what they wanted meant death on a larger scale. He nodded his head from side to side.

"For you to already have that picture of my family means they're already dead." Shukre struggled to swallow the huge lump in his throat. Allowing himself time to fix his mouth with the right words he finished, "When you reach hell, I'll be waiting for ya, you bitch ass muthafucka!"

He died seconds later as the taller man choked him on his own spittle.

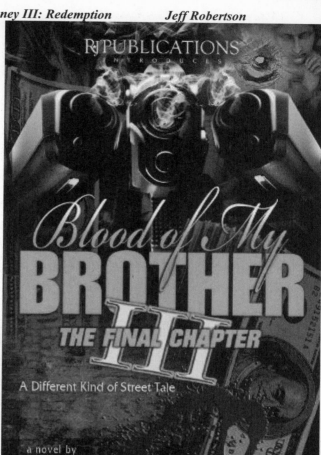

Retiring is no longer an option for Roc, who is now forced to restudy Philly's vicious streets through blood filled eyes. He realizes that his brother's killer is none other than his mentor, Mr. Holmes. With this knowledge, the strategic game of chess that began with the pushing of a pawn in the Blood of My Brother series, symbolizes one of love, loyalty, blood, mayhem, and death. In the end, the streets of Philadelphia will never be the same...

In Storess!!!

After Chasin' Satisfaction, Julius finds that satisfaction is not all that it's cracked up to be. It left nothing but death in its aftermath. Now living the glamorous life in Miami while putting the finishing touches on his hybrid condo hotel, he realizes with newfound success he's now become the hunted. Julian's success is threatened as someone from his past vows revenge on him.

In Stores!!!

It may not be Histeria Lane, but these desperate housewives are fed up with their neglecting husbands. Their sexual needs take precedence over the millions of dollars their husbands bring home every year to keep them happy in their affluent neighborhood. While their husbands claim to be hard at work, these wives are doing a little work of their own with the bedroom bandit. Is the bandit swift enough to evade these angry husbands?

In Stores!!

NEGLECTED SOULS

Motherhood and the trials of loving too hard and not enough frame this story...The realism of these characters will bring tears to your spirit as you discover the hero in the villain you never saw coming...

In Stores!!!

Jimmy and Nina continue to feel a void in their lives because they haven't a clue about their genealogical make-up. Jimmy falls victims to a life threatening illness and only the right organ donor can save his life. Will the donor be the bridge to reconnect Jimmy and Nina to their biological family? Will Nina be the strength for her brother in his time of need? Will they ever find out what really happened to their mother?

In Stores!!!

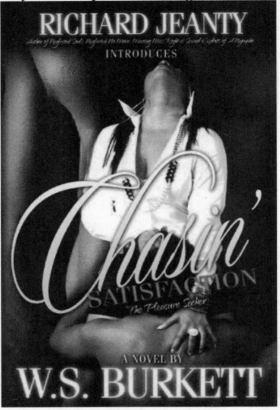

Betrayal, lust, lies, murder, deception, sex and tainted love frame this story... Julian Stevens lacks the ambition and freak ability that Miko looks for in a man, but she married him despite his flaws to spite an ex-boyfriend. When Miko least expects it, the old boyfriend shows up and ready to sweep her off her feet again. She wants to have her cake and eat it too. While Miko's doing her own thing, Julian is determined to become everything Miko ever wanted in a man and more, but will he go to extreme lengths to prove he's worthy of Miko's love? Julian Stevens soon finds out that he's capable of being more than he could ever imagine as he embarks on a journey that will change his life forever.

In Stores!!!

The police in New York and other major cities around the country are increasingly victimizing black men. The violence has escalated to deadly force, most of the time without justification. In this controversial book, noted author Richard Jeanty, tackles the problem of police brutality and the unfair treatment of Black men at the hands of police in New York City and the rest of the country.

In Stores!!!

Just when Darren thinks his relationship with Tina is flourishing, there is yet another hurdle on the road hindering their bliss. Tina saw a therapist for months to deal with her sexual addiction, but now Darren is wondering if she was ever treated completely. Darren has not been taking care of home and Tina's frustrated and agrees to a break-up with Darren. Will Darren lose Tina for good? Will Tina ever realize that Darren is the best man for her?

In Stores!!

Ronald Murphy was a player all his life until he and his best friend, Myles, met the women of their dreams during a brief vacation in South Beach, Florida. Sexual Jeopardy is story of trust, betrayal, forgiveness, friendship and hope.
In Stores!!!

Tina develops an insatiable sexual appetite very early in life. She
only loves her boyfriend, Darren, but he's too far away in college to satisfy her sexual needs.
Tina decides to get buck wild away in college
Will her sexual trysts jeopardize the lives of the men in her life?

In Stores!!!

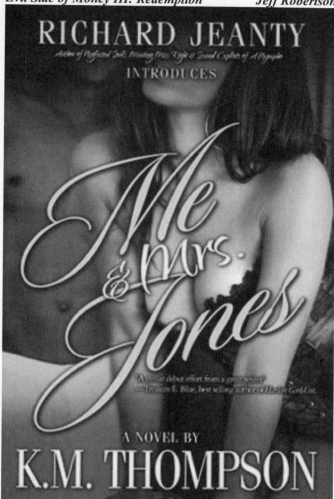

Faith Jones, a woman in her mid-thirties, has given up on ever finding love again until she met her son's best friend, Darius. Faith Jones is walking a thin line of betrayal against her son for the love of Darius. Will Faith allow her emotions to outweigh her common sense?

In Stores!!!

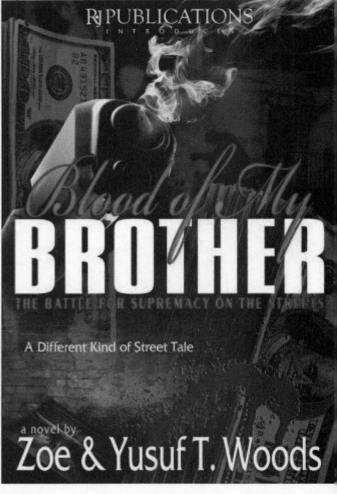

Roc was the man on the streets of Philadelphia, until his younger brother decided it was time to become his own man by wreaking havoc on Roc's crew without any regards for the blood relation they share. Drug, murder, mayhem and the pursuit of happiness can lead to deadly consequences. This story can only be told by a person who has lived it.

In Stores!!!

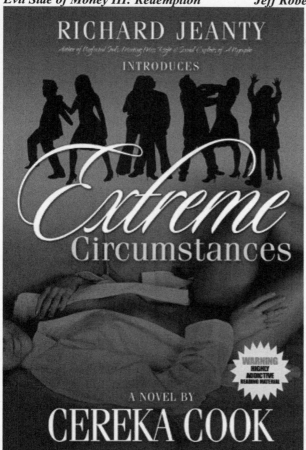

What happens when a devoted woman is betrayed? Come take a ride with Chanel as she takes her boyfriend, Donnell, to circumstances beyond belief after he betrays her trust with his endless infidelities. How long can Chanel's friend, Janai, use her looks to get what she wants from men before it catches up to her? Find out as Janai's gold-digging ways catch up with and she has to face the consequences of her extreme actions.

In Stores!!!

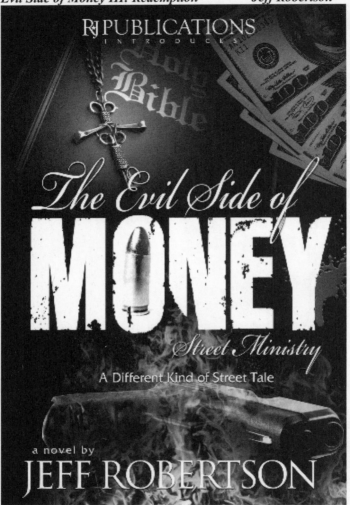

Violence, Intimidation and carnage are the order as Nathan and his brother set out to build the most powerful drug empires in Chicago. However, when God comes knocking, Nathan's conscience starts to surface. Will his haunted criminal past get the best of him?

In Stores!!

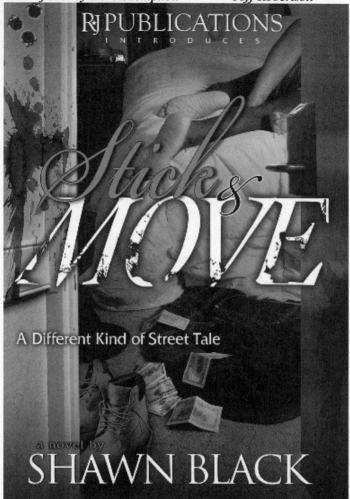

RJ PUBLICATIONS
I N T R O D U C E S

Stick &
MOVE

A Different Kind of Street Tale

a novel by
SHAWN BLACK

Yasmina witnessed the brutal murder of her parents at a
young age at the hand of a drug dealer. This event stained
her mind and upbringing as a result. Will Yamina's life
come full circle with her past? Find out as Yasmina's crew,
The Platinum Chicks, set out to make a name for themselves
on the street.

In stores!!

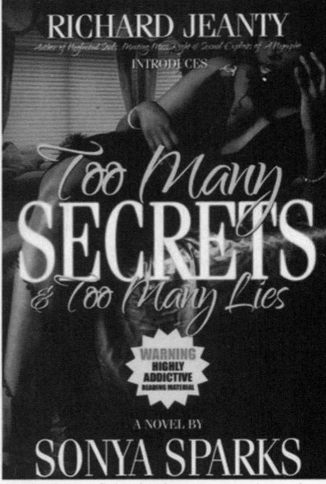

RICHARD JEANTY
Author of Neglected Souls, Meeting Miss Right & Sexual Exploits of A Nympho
INTRODUCES

Too Many
SECRETS
& Too Many Lies

WARNING
HIGHLY
ADDICTIVE
READING MATERIAL

A NOVEL BY
SONYA SPARKS

Ashland's mother, Bianca, fights hard to suppress the truth from her daughter because she doesn't want her to marry Jordan, the grandson of an ex-lover she loathes. Ashland soon finds out how cruel and vengeful her mother can be, but what price will Bianca pay for redemption?

In stores!!

Malcolm is a wealthy virgin who decides to conceal his wealth From the world until he meets the right woman. His wealthy best friend, Dexter, hides his wealth from no one. Malcolm struggles to find love in an environment where vanity and materialism are rampant, while Dexter is getting more than enough of his share of women. Malcolm needs develop self-esteem and confidence to meet the right woman and Dexter's confidence is borderline arrogance.
Will bad boys like Dexter continue to take women for a ride?

Or will nice guys like Malcolm continue to finish last?

In Stores!!!

What happens when a woman's devotion to her fiancee is tested weeks before she gets married? What if her fiancee is just hiding behind the veil of ministry to deceive her? Find out as Sean Mitchell takes you on a journey you'll never forget into the lives of Angelica, Titus and Aurelius.

In Stores!!

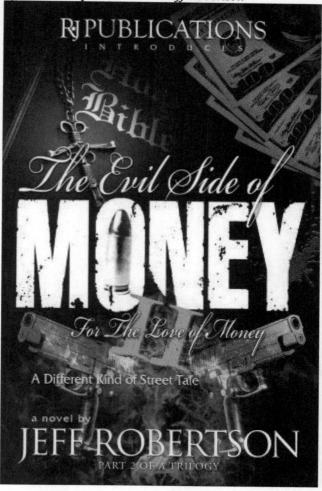

A beautigul woman from Bolivia threatens the existence of the drug empire that Nate and G have built. While Nate is head over heels for her, G can see right through her. As she brings on more conflict between the crew, G sets out to show Nate exactly who she is before she brings about their demise.

In Stores!!!

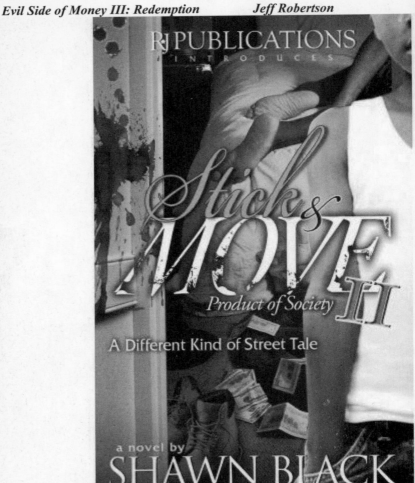

Scorcher and Yasmina's low key lifestyle was interrupted when they were taken down by the Feds, but their daughter, Serosa, was left to be raised by the foster care system. Will Serosa become a product of her environment or will she rise above it all? Her bloodline is undeniable, but will she be able to control it?

In Stores!!

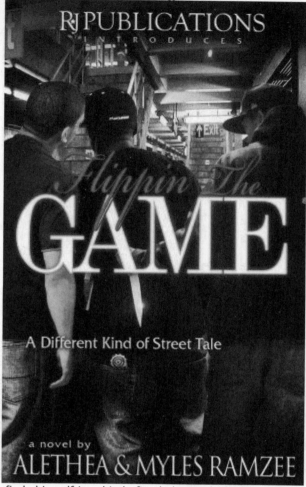

An ex-drug dealer finds himself in a bind after he's caught by the Feds. He has to decide which is more important, his family or his loyalty to the game. As he fights hard to make a decision, those who helped him to the top fear the worse from him. Will he get the chance to tell the govt. whole story, or will someone get to him before he becomes a snitch?

In Stores!!!

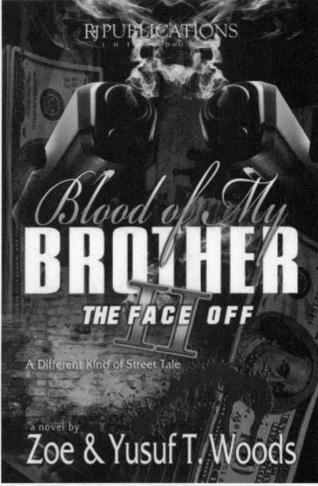

What will Roc do when he finds out the true identity of Solo? Will the blood shed come from his own brother Lil Mac? Will Roc and Solo take their beef to an explosive height on the street? Find out as Zoe and Yusuf bring the second installment to their hot street joint, Blood of My Brother.

In Stores!!!

Dave Richardson is enjoying success as his second book became a New York Times best-seller. He left the life of The Bedroom behind to settle with his family, but an obsessed fan has not had enough of Dave and she will go to great length to get a piece of him. How far will a woman go to get a man that doesn't belong to her?

Coming September 2010

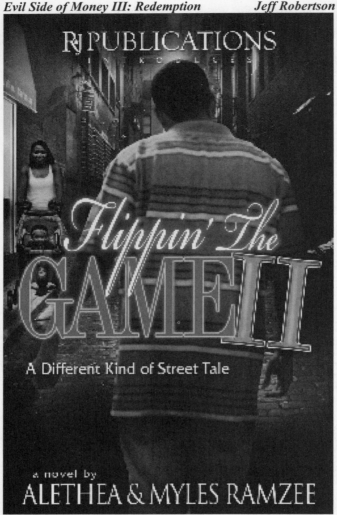

Nafys Muhammad managed to beat the charges in court, but will he beat them on the street? There will be many revelations in this story as betrayal, greed, sex scandal corruption and murder unravels throughout every page. Get ready for a rough ride.

Coming December 2009

Deon is at the mercy of a ruthless gang that kidnapped him. In a foreign land where he knows nothing about the culture, he has to use his survival instincts and his wit to outsmart his captors. Will the Hoodfellas show up in time to rescue Deon, or will Crazy D take over once again and fight an all out war by himself?

Coming March 2010

While Yasmina sits on death row awaiting her fate, her daughter, Serosa, is fighting the fight of her life on the outside. Her genetic structure that indirectly bins her to her parents could also be her downfall and force her to see that there's no way out!

Coming January 2010

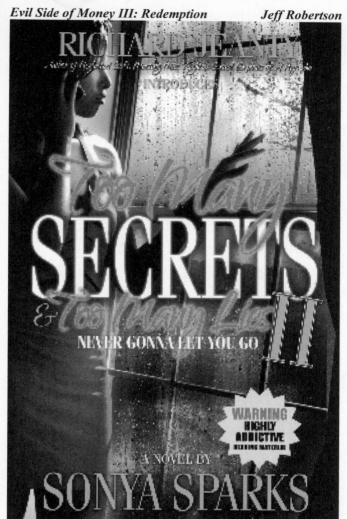

The drama continues as Deshun is hunted by Angela who still feels that ex-girlfriend Kayla is still trying to win his heart, though he brutally raped her. Angela will kill anyone who gets in her way, but is DeShun worth all the aggravation?

In Stores!!!

Buck Johnson was forced to make the best out of worst situation. He has witnessed the most cruel events in his life and it is those events who the man that he has become. Was the Johnson family ignorant souls through no fault of their own?

In Stores!!!

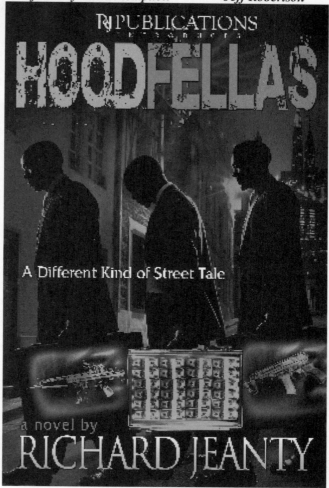

When an Ex-con finds himself destitute and in dire need of the basic necessities after he's released from prison, he turns to what he knows best, crime, but at what cost? Extortion, murder and mayhem drives him back to the top, but will he stay there?

In Stores !!!

RICHARD JEANTY

Author of Neglected Souls, Meeting Miss Right & Sexual Exploits of a Nympho

INTRODUCES

Insanely
IN
Love

WARNING
HIGHLY
ADDICTIVE
READING MATERIAL

A NOVEL BY

CEREKA COOK

Author of *Extreme Circumstances*

What happens when someone falls insanely in love?
Stalking is just the beginning.
In Stores!!!

Use this coupon to order by mail

1. Neglected Souls, Richard Jeanty $14.95
2. Neglected No More, Richard Jeanty $14.95
3. Ignorant Souls, Richard Jeanty $15.00, October 2009
4. Sexual Exploits of Nympho, Richard Jeanty $14.95
5. Meeting Ms. Right's Whip Appeal, Richard Jeanty $14.95
6. Me and Mrs. Jones, K.M Thompson $14.95
7. Chasin' Satisfaction, W.S Burkett $14.95
8. Extreme Circumstances, Cereka Cook $14.95
9. The Most Dangerous Gang In America, R. Jeanty $15.00
10. Sexual Exploits of a Nympho II, Richard Jeanty $15.00
11. Sexual Jeopardy, Richard Jeanty $14.95
12. Too Many Secrets, Too Many Lies, Sonya Sparks $15.00
13. Stick And Move, Shawn Black $15.00 Available
14. Evil Side Of Money, Jeff Robertson $15.00
15. Evil Side Of Money II, Jeff Robertson $15.00
16. Evil Side Of Money III, Jeff Robertson $15.00
17. Flippin' The Game, Alethea and M. Ramzee, $15.00 Available
18. Flippin' The Game II, Alethea and M. Ramzee, $15.00 Dec. 2009
19. Cater To Her, W.S Burkett $15.00
20. Blood of My Brother I, Zoe & Yusuf Woods $15.00
21. Blood of my Brother II, Zoe & Ysuf Woods $15.00
22. Hoodfellas, Richard Jeanty $15.00 available
23. Hoodfellas II, Richard Jeanty, $15.00 03/30/2010
24. The Bedroom Bandit, Richard Jeanty $15.00 Available
25. Mr. Erotica, Richard Jeanty, $15.00, Sept 2010
26. Stick N Move II, Shawn Black $15.00 Available
27. Stick N Move III, Shawn Black $15.00 Jan, 2010
28. Miami Noire, W.S. Burkett $15.00 Available
29. Insanely In Love, Cereka Cook $15.00 Available
30. Blood of My Brother III, Zoe & Yusuf Woods September 2009

Name_____

Address_____

City_____State_____Zip Code_____

Please send the novels that I have circled above.

Shipping and Handling: Free

Total Number of Books_____

Total Amount Due_____

Buy 3 books and get 1 free. This offer is subject to change without notice.

Send institution check or money order (no cash or CODs) to:

RJ Publications

PO Box 300771

Jamaica, NY 11434

For more information please call 718-471-2926, or visit www.rjpublications.com

Please allow 2-3 weeks for delivery.

Use this coupon to order by mail

31. Neglected Souls, Richard Jeanty $14.95
32. Neglected No More, Richard Jeanty $14.95
33. Ignorant Souls, Richard Jeanty $15.00, October 2009
34. Sexual Exploits of Nympho, Richard Jeanty $14.95
35. Meeting Ms. Right's Whip Appeal, Richard Jeanty $14.95
36. Me and Mrs. Jones, K.M Thompson $14.95
37. Chasin' Satisfaction, W.S Burkett $14.95
38. Extreme Circumstances, Cereka Cook $14.95
39. The Most Dangerous Gang In America, R. Jeanty $15.00
40. Sexual Exploits of a Nympho II, Richard Jeanty $15.00
41. Sexual Jeopardy, Richard Jeanty $14.95
42. Too Many Secrets, Too Many Lies, Sonya Sparks $15.00
43. Stick And Move, Shawn Black $15.00 Available
44. Evil Side Of Money, Jeff Robertson $15.00
45. Evil Side Of Money II, Jeff Robertson $15.00
46. Evil Side Of Money III, Jeff Robertson $15.00
47. Flippin' The Game, Alethea and M. Ramzee, $15.00 Available
48. Flippin' The Game II, Alethea and M. Ramzee, $15.00 Dec. 2009
49. Cater To Her, W.S Burkett $15.00
50. Blood of My Brother I, Zoe & Yusuf Woods $15.00
51. Blood of my Brother II, Zoe & Ysuf Woods $15.00
52. Hoodfellas, Richard Jeanty $15.00 available
53. Hoodfellas II, Richard Jeanty, $15.00 03/30/2010
54. The Bedroom Bandit, Richard Jeanty $15.00 Available
55. Mr. Erotica, Richard Jeanty, $15.00, Sept 2010
56. Stick N Move II, Shawn Black $15.00 Available
57. Stick N Move III, Shawn Black $15.00 Jan, 2010
58. Miami Noire, W.S. Burkett $15.00 Available
59. Insanely In Love, Cereka Cook $15.00 Available
60. Blood of My Brother III, Zoe & Yusuf Woods September 2009

Name_____

Address_____

City_____State_____Zip Code_____

Please send the novels that I have circled above.
Shipping and Handling: Free
Total Number of Books_____
Total Amount Due_____
Buy 3 books and get 1 free. This offer is subject to change without notice.
Send institution check or money order (no cash or CODs) to:
RJ Publications
PO Box 300771
Jamaica, NY 11434
For more information please call 718-471-2926, or visit www.rjpublications.com

Please allow 2-3 weeks for delivery.

Use this coupon to order by mail

61. Neglected Souls, Richard Jeanty $14.95
62. Neglected No More, Richard Jeanty $14.95
63. Ignorant Souls, Richard Jeanty $15.00, October 2009
64. Sexual Exploits of Nympho, Richard Jeanty $14.95
65. Meeting Ms. Right's Whip Appeal, Richard Jeanty $14.95
66. Me and Mrs. Jones, K.M Thompson $14.95
67. Chasin' Satisfaction, W.S Burkett $14.95
68. Extreme Circumstances, Cereka Cook $14.95
69. The Most Dangerous Gang In America, R. Jeanty $15.00
70. Sexual Exploits of a Nympho II, Richard Jeanty $15.00
71. Sexual Jeopardy, Richard Jeanty $14.95
72. Too Many Secrets, Too Many Lies, Sonya Sparks $15.00
73. Stick And Move, Shawn Black $15.00 Available
74. Evil Side Of Money, Jeff Robertson $15.00
75. Evil Side Of Money II, Jeff Robertson $15.00
76. Evil Side Of Money III, Jeff Robertson $15.00
77. Flippin' The Game, Alethea and M. Ramzee, $15.00 Available
78. Flippin' The Game II, Alethea and M. Ramzee, $15.00 Dec. 2009
79. Cater To Her, W.S Burkett $15.00
80. Blood of My Brother I, Zoe & Yusuf Woods $15.00
81. Blood of my Brother II, Zoe & Ysuf Woods $15.00
82. Hoodfellas, Richard Jeanty $15.00 available
83. Hoodfellas II, Richard Jeanty, $15.00 03/30/2010
84. The Bedroom Bandit, Richard Jeanty $15.00 Available
85. Mr. Erotica, Richard Jeanty, $15.00, Sept 2010
86. Stick N Move II, Shawn Black $15.00 Available
87. Stick N Move III, Shawn Black $15.00 Jan, 2010
88. Miami Noire, W.S. Burkett $15.00 Available
89. Insanely In Love, Cereka Cook $15.00 Available
90. Blood of My Brother III, Zoe & Yusuf Woods September 2009

Name_____

Address_____

City_____State_____Zip Code_____

Please send the novels that I have circled above.

Shipping and Handling: Free

Total Number of Books_____

Total Amount Due_____

Buy 3 books and get 1 free. This offer is subject to change without notice.
Send institution check or money order (no cash or CODs) to:

RJ Publications

PO Box 300771

Jamaica, NY 11434

For more information please call 718-471-2926, or visit www.rjpublications.com

Please allow 2-3 weeks for delivery.